W9-BTH-361

From an etching by Férat VI

THE PIT AND THE PENDULUM

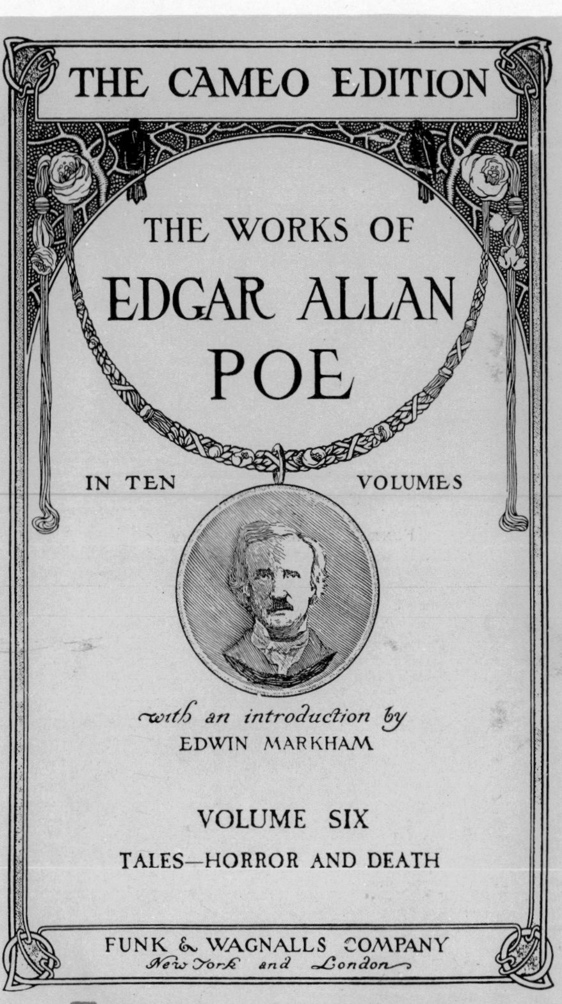

THE CAMEO EDITION

THE WORKS OF EDGAR ALLAN POE

IN TEN VOLUMES

with an introduction by
EDWIN MARKHAM

VOLUME SIX

TALES—HORROR AND DEATH

FUNK & WAGNALLS COMPANY
New York and London

VOLUME VI

TALES—HORROR AND DEATH *

CONTENTS

* See also, "The Oblong Box," Vol. III, and "The Masque of the Red Death," Vol. VII.

THE PIT AND THE PENDULUM

[Published in *The Gift*, 1843.]

Impia tortorum longos hic turba furores
Sanguinis innocui, non satiata, aluit.
Sospite nunc patriâ, fracto nunc funeris antro,
Mors ubi dira fuit vita salusque patent.

[*Quatrain composed for the gates of a market to be erected upon the site of the Jacobin Club House at Paris.*]

I WAS sick—sick unto death with that long agony; and when they at length unbound me, and I was permitted to sit, I felt that my senses were leaving me. The sentence—the dread sentence of death—was the last of distinct accentuation which reached my ears. After that, the sound of the inquisitorial voices seemed merged in one dreamy indeterminate hum. It conveyed to my soul the idea of *revolution*—perhaps from its association in fancy with the burr of a millwheel. This only for a brief period, for presently I heard no more. Yet, for a while, I saw—but with how terrible an exaggeration! I saw the lips of the black-robed judges. They appeared to me white—whiter than the sheet upon which I trace these words—and thin even to grotesqueness; thin with the intensity of their expression of firmness—of immovable resolution—of stern contempt of human torture. I saw that the decrees of what to me was Fate were still issuing from those lips. I saw them writhe with a deadly locution. I saw them fashion the syllables of my name; and I shuddered because no sound succeeded. I saw, too, for a few moments of delirious horror, the soft and nearly imperceptible waving of the sable draperies which enwrapped the walls of the apartment. And then my vision fell upon the seven tall candles upon the table. At first they wore the aspect of charity, and seemed white slender angels who would save me; but then, all at once, there came a most deadly nausea over my spirit, and I felt every fibre in my frame thrill as if I had touched the wire of a galvanic battery, while the angel forms became meaningless spectres, with heads of flame, and I saw that from them there would be no help. And then there stole into my fancy, like a rich musical note, the thought of what sweet rest there must be in the grave. The thought came gently and stealthily, and it seemed long before it attained full appreciation; but just as my spirit came at length properly to feel and entertain it, the figures of the judges vanished, as if magically, from before me; the tall candles sank into nothingness; their flames went out utterly; the blackness of darkness supervened; all sensations appeared swallowed up in a mad rushing descent as of the soul into Hades. Then silence, and stillness, and night were the universe.

I had swooned; but still will not say that all of consciousness was lost. What of it there remained I will not attempt to define, or even to describe; yet all was not lost. In the deepest slumber—no! In delirium—no! In a swoon—no! In death—no! even in the grave all *is not* lost. Else there is no immortality for man. Arousing from the most profound of slumbers, we break the gossamer web of *some* dream. Yet in a second afterward, (so frail may that web have been) we remember not that we have dreamed. In the return to life from the swoon there are two stages: first, that of the sense of mental or spiritual; secondly, that of the sense of physical, existence. It seems probable that if, upon reaching the second stage, we could recall the impressions of the first, we should find these impressions eloquent in memories of the gulf beyond. And that gulf is—what? How at least shall we distinguish its shadows from those of the tomb? But if the impressions of what I have termed the first stage are not, at will, recalled, yet, after long interval, do they not come unbidden, while we marvel whence they come? He who has never swooned, is not he who finds strange palaces and wildly familiar faces in coals that glow; is not he who beholds floating in mid-air the sad visions that the many may not view; is not he who ponders over the perfume of some novel flower; is not he whose brain grows bewildered with the meaning of some musical cadence which has never before arrested his attention.

Amid frequent and thoughtful endeavors to

remember, amid earnest struggles to regather some token of the state of seeming nothingness into which my soul had lapsed, there have been moments when I have dreamed of success; there have been brief, very brief periods when I have conjured up remembrances which the lucid reason of a later epoch assures me could have had reference only to that condition of seeming unconsciousness. These shadows of memory tell, indistinctly, of tall figures that lifted and bore me in silence down—down—still down—till a hideous dizziness oppressed me at the mere idea of the interminableness of the descent. They tell also of a vague horror at my heart, on account of that heart's unnatural stillness. Then comes a sense of sudden motionlessness throughout all things; as if those who bore me (a ghastly train!) had outrun, in their descent, the limits of the limitless, and paused from the wearisomeness of their toil. After this I call to mind flatness and dampness; and then all is *madness*—the madness of a memory which busies itself among forbidden things.

Very suddenly there came back to my soul motion and sound—the tumultuous motion of the heart, and, in my ears, the sound of its beating. Then a pause in which all is blank. Then again sound, and motion, and touch—a tingling sensation pervading my frame. Then the mere consciousness of existence, without thought—a condition which lasted long. Then, very suddenly, *thought*, and shuddering terror, and earnest endeavor to comprehend my true state. Then a strong desire to lapse into insensibility. Then a rushing revival of soul and a successful effort to move. And now a full memory of the trial, of the judges, of the sable draperies, of the sentence, of the sickness, of the swoon. Then entire forgetfulness of all that followed; of all that a later day and much earnestness of endeavor have enabled me vaguely to recall.

So far, I had not opened my eyes. I felt that I lay upon my back, unbound. I reached out my hand, and it fell heavily upon something damp and hard. There I suffered it to remain for many minutes, while I strove to imagine where and *what* I could be. I longed, dared not, to employ my vision. I dreaded the first glance at objects around me. It was not that I feared to look upon things horrible, but that I grew aghast lest there should be *nothing* to see. At length, with a wild desperation at heart, I quickly unclosed my eyes. My worst thoughts, then, were confirmed. The blackness of eternal night encompassed me. I struggled for breath. The intensity of the darkness seemed to oppress and stifle me. The atmosphere was intolerably close. I still lay quietly, and made effort to exercise my reason. I brought to mind the inquisitorial proceedings, and attempted from that point to deduce my real condition. The sentence had passed; and it appeared to me that a very long interval of time had since elapsed. Yet not for a moment did I suppose myself actually dead. Such a supposition, notwithstanding what we read in fiction, is altogether inconsistent with real existence;—but where and in what state was I? The condemned to death, I knew, perished usually at the *autos-da-fé,* and one of these had been held on the very night of the day of my trial. Had I been remanded to my dungeon, to await the next sacrifice, which would not take place for many months? This I at once saw could not be. Victims had been in immediate demand. Moreover, my dungeon, as well as all the condemned cells at Toledo, had stone floors, and light was not altogether excluded.

A fearful idea now suddenly drove the blood in torrents upon my heart, and for a brief period I once more relapsed into insensibility. Upon recovering, I at once started to my feet, trembling convulsively in every fibre. I thrust my arms wildly above and around me in all directions. I felt nothing; yet dreaded to move a step, lest I should be impeded by the walls of a *tomb.* Perspiration burst from every pore, and stood in cold big beads upon my forehead. The agony of suspense grew at length intolerable, and I cautiously moved forward, with my arms extended, and my eyes straining from their sockets in the hope of catching some faint ray of light. I proceeded for many paces; but still all was blackness and vacancy. I breathed more freely. It seemed evident that mine was not, at least, the most hideous of fates.

And now, as I still continued to step cautiously onward, there came thronging upon my recollection a thousand vague rumors of the horrors of Toledo. Of the dungeons there had been strange things narrated—fables I had always deemed them,—but yet strange, and too ghastly to repeat, save in a whisper. Was I left to perish of starvation in the subterranean world of darkness; or what fate, perhaps even more fearful, awaited me? That the result would be death, and a death of more than customary bitterness, I knew too well the character of my judges to doubt. The mode and the hour were all that occupied or distracted me.

My outstretched hands at length encountered some solid obstruction. It was a wall, seemingly of stone masonry—very smooth, slimy, and cold. I followed it up; stepping with all the careful distrust with which certain antique narratives had inspired me. This process, however, afforded me no means of ascertaining the dimensions of my dungeon, as I might make its circuit and return to the point whence I set out without being aware of the fact, so perfectly uniform seemed the wall. I therefore sought the knife which had been in my pocket when led into the inquisitorial chamber; but it was gone; my clothes had been exchanged for a wrapper of coarse serge. I had thought of forcing the blade in some minute crevice of the masonry, so as to identify my point of departure. The difficulty, nevertheless, was but trivial; although, in the disorder of my fancy, it seemed at first insuperable. I tore a part of the hem from the robe and placed the fragment at full length, and at right angles to the wall. In groping my way around the prison, I could not fail to encounter this rag upon completing the circuit. So, at least, I thought; but I had not counted upon the extent of the dungeon, or upon my own weakness. The ground was moist and slippery. I staggered onward for some time, when I stumbled and fell. My excessive fatigue induced me to remain prostrate; and sleep soon overtook me as I lay.

Upon awaking, and stretching forth an arm, I found beside me a loaf and a pitcher with water. I was too much exhausted to reflect upon this circumstance, but ate and drank with avidity. Shortly afterward, I resumed my tour around the prison, and with much toil, came at last upon the fragment of the serge. Up to the period when I fell, I had counted fifty-two paces, and, upon resuming my walk, I had counted forty-eight more—when I arrived at the rag. There were in all, then, a hundred paces; and, admitting two paces to the yard, I presumed the dungeon to be fifty yards in circuit. I had met, however, with many angles in the wall, and thus I could form no guess at the shape of the vault, for vault I could not help supposing it to be.

I had little object—certainly no hope—in these researches; but a vague curiosity prompted me to continue them. Quitting the wall, I resolved to cross the area of the enclosure. At first, I proceeded with extreme caution, for the floor, although seemingly of solid material, was treacherous with slime. At length, however, I took courage, and did not hesitate to step firmly—endeavoring to cross in as direct a line as possible. I had advanced some ten or twelve paces in this manner, when the remnant of the torn hem of my robe became entangled between my legs. I stepped on it, and fell violently on my face.

In the confusion attending my fall, I did not immediately apprehend a somewhat startling circumstance, which yet, in a few seconds afterward, and while I still lay prostrate, arrested my attention. It was this: my chin rested upon the floor of the prison, but my lips, and the upper portion of my head, although seemingly at a less elevation than the chin, touched nothing. At the same time, my forehead seemed bathed in a clammy vapor, and the peculiar smell of decayed fungus arose to my nostrils. I put forward my arm, and shuddered to find that I had fallen at the very brink of a circular pit, whose extent, of course, I had no means of ascertaining at the moment. Groping about the masonry just below the margin, I succeeded in dislodging a small fragment, and let it fall into the abyss. For many seconds I hearkened to its reverberations as it dashed against the sides of the chasm in its descent; at length, there was a sullen plunge into water, succeeded by loud echoes. At the same moment, there came a sound resembling the quick opening and as rapid closing of a door overhead, while a faint gleam of light flashed suddenly through the gloom, and as suddenly faded away.

I saw clearly the doom which had been prepared for me, and congratulated myself upon the timely accident by which I had escaped. Another step before my fall, and the world had seen me no more. And the death just avoided was of that very character which I had regarded as fabulous and frivolous in the tales respecting the Inquisition. To the victims of its tyranny, there was the choice of death with its direst physical agonies, or death with its most hideous moral horrors. I had been reserved for the latter. By long suffering my nerves had been unstrung, until I trembled at the sound of my own voice, and had become in every respect a fitting subject for the species of torture which awaited me.

Shaking in every limb, I groped my way back to the wall—resolving there to perish rather than risk the terrors of the wells, of which my imagination now pictured many in various positions about the dungeon. In other conditions of mind, I might have had courage to end my misery at once, by a plunge into one of these abysses; but now I was the veriest of cowards. Neither could I forget what I had read of these pits—that the *sudden* extinction of life formed no part of their most horrible plan.

Agitation of spirit kept me awake for many long hours, but at length I again slumbered. Upon arousing, I found by my side, as before, a loaf and a pitcher of water. A burning thirst consumed me, and I emptied the vessel at a draught. It must have been drugged—for scarcely had I drunk, before I became irresistibly drowsy. A deep sleep fell upon me—a sleep like that of death. How long it lasted, of course I know not; but when, once again, I unclosed my eyes, the objects around me were visible. By a wild, sulphurous lustre, the origin of which I could not at first determine, I was enabled to see the extent and aspect of the prison.

In its size I had been greatly mistaken. The whole circuit of its walls did not exceed twenty-five yards. For some minutes this fact occasioned me a world of vain trouble; vain indeed—for what could be of less importance, under the terrible circumstances which environed me, than the mere dimensions of my dungeon? But my soul took a wild interest in trifles, and I busied myself in endeavors to account for the error I had committed in my measurement. The truth at length flashed upon me. In my first attempt at exploration I had counted fifty-two paces, up to the period when I fell: I must then have been within a pace or two of the fragment of serge; in fact, I had nearly performed the circuit of the vault. I then slept—and, upon awaking, I must have returned upon my steps—thus supposing the circuit nearly double what it actually was. My confusion of mind prevented me from observing that I began my tour with the wall to the left, and ended it with the wall to the right.

I had been deceived, too, in respect to the shape of the enclosure. In feeling my way I had found many angles, and thus deduced an idea of great irregularity; so potent is the effect of total darkness upon one arousing from lethargy or sleep! The angles were simply those of a few slight depressions, or niches, at odd intervals. The general shape of the prison was square. What I had taken for masonry seemed now to be iron, or some other metal, in huge plates, whose sutures or joints occasioned the depression. The entire surface of this metallic enclosure was rudely daubed in all the hideous and repulsive devices to which the charnel superstition of the monks has given rise. The figures of fiends in aspects of menace, with skeleton forms, and other more really fearful images, overspread and disfigured the walls. I observed that the outlines of these monstrosities were sufficiently distinct, but that the colors seemed faded and blurred, as if from the effects of a damp atmosphere. I now noticed the floor, too, which was of stone. In the centre yawned the circular pit from whose jaws I had escaped; but it was the only one in the dungeon.

All this I saw indistinctly and by much effort —for my personal condition had been greatly changed during slumber. I now lay upon my back, and at full length, on a species of low framework of wood. To this I was securely bound by a long strap resembling a surcingle. It passed in many convolutions about my limbs and body, leaving at liberty only my head, and my left arm to such an extent, that I could, by dint of much exertion, supply myself with food from an earthen dish which lay by my side on the floor. I saw, to my horror, that the pitcher had been removed. I say to my horror—for I was consumed with intolerable thirst. This thirst it appeared to be the design of my persecutors to stimulate—for the food in the dish was meat pungently seasoned.

Looking upward, I surveyed the ceiling of my prison. It was some thirty or forty feet overhead, and constructed much as the side walls. In one of its panels a very singular figure riveted my whole attention. It was the painted figure of Time as he is commonly represented, save that, in lieu of a scythe, he held what, at a casual glance, I supposed to be the pictured image of a huge pendulum, such as we see on antique clocks. There was something, however, in the appearance of this machine which caused me to regard it more attentively. While I gazed directly upward at it (for its position was immediately over my own) I fancied that I saw it in motion. In an instant afterward the fancy was confirmed. Its sweep was brief, and of course slow. I watched it for some minutes somewhat in fear, but more in wonder. Wearied at length with observing its dull movement, I turned my eyes upon the other objects in the cell.

A slight noise attracted my notice, and, looking to the floor, I saw several enormous rats traversing it. They had issued from the well which lay just within view to my right. Even then, while I gazed, they came up in troops, hurriedly, with ravenous eyes, allured by the scent of the meat. From this it required much effort and attention to scare them away.

It might have been half an hour, perhaps, even an hour (for I could take but imperfect note of time), before I again cast my eyes upward. What

I then saw confounded and amazed me. The sweep of the pendulum had increased in extent by nearly a yard. As a natural consequence its velocity was also much greater. But what mainly disturbed me was the idea that it had perceptibly *descended.* I now observed—with what horror it is needless to say—that its nether extremity was formed of a crescent of glittering steel, about a foot in length from horn to horn; the horns upward, and the under edge evidently as keen as that of a razor. Like a razor also, it seemed massy and heavy, tapering from the edge into a solid and broad structure above. It was appended to a weighty rod of brass, and the whole *hissed* as it swung through the air.

I could no longer doubt the doom prepared for me by monkish ingenuity in torture. My cognizance of the pit had become known to the inquisitorial agents—*the pit,* whose horrors had been destined for so bold a recusant as myself—*the pit,* typical of hell and regarded by rumor as the Ultima Thule of all their punishments. The plunge into this pit I had avoided by the merest of accidents, and I knew that surprise, or entrapment into torment, formed an important portion of all the grotesquerie of these dungeon deaths. Having failed to fall, it was no part of the demon plan to hurl me into the abyss, and thus (there being no alternative) a different and a milder destruction awaited me. Milder! I half smiled in my agony as I thought of such application of such a term.

What boots it to tell of the long, long hours

of horror more than mortal, during which I counted the rushing oscillations of the steel! Inch by inch—line by line—with a descent only appreciable at intervals that seemed ages—down and still down it came! Days passed—it might have been that many days passed—ere it swept so closely over me as to fan me with its acrid breath. The odor of the sharp steel forced itself into my nostrils. I prayed—I wearied heaven with my prayer for its more speedy descent. I grew frantically mad, and struggled to force myself upward against the sweep of the fearful scimitar. And then I fell suddenly calm, and lay smiling at the glittering death, as a child at some rare bauble.

There was another interval of utter insensibility; it was brief; for, upon again lapsing into life, there had been no perceptible descent in the pendulum. But it might have been long—for I knew there were demons who took note of my swoon, and who could have arrested the vibration at pleasure. Upon my recovery, too, I felt very—oh! inexpressibly—sick and weak, as if through long inanition. Even amid the agonies of that period, the human nature craved food. With painful effort I outstretched my left arm as far as my bonds permitted, and took possession of the small remnant which had been spared me by the rats. As I put a portion of it within my lips, there rushed to my mind a half-formed thought of joy—of hope. Yet what business had *I* with hope? It was, as I say, a half-formed thought—man has many such, which are never completed. I felt that it was of joy—of hope; but I felt also that it had perished in its formation. In vain I struggled to perfect—to regain it. Long suffering had nearly annihilated all my ordinary powers of mind. I was an imbecile—an idiot.

The vibration of the pendulum was at right angles to my length. I saw that the crescent was designed to cross the region of the heart. It would fray the serge of my robe—it would return and repeat its operations—again—and again. Notwithstanding its terrifically wide sweep (some thirty feet or more), and the hissing vigor of its descent, sufficient to sunder these very walls of iron, still the fraying of my robe would be all that, for several minutes, it would accomplish. And at this thought I paused. I dared not go further than this reflection. I dwelt upon it with a pertinacity of attention—as if, in so dwelling, I could arrest *here* the descent of the steel. I forced myself to ponder upon the sound of the crescent as it should pass across the garment—upon the peculiar thrilling sensation which the friction of cloth produces on the nerves. I pondered upon all this frivolity until my teeth were on edge.

Down—steadily down it crept. I took a frenzied pleasure in contrasting its downward with its lateral velocity. To the right—to the left—far and wide—with the shriek of a damned spirit! to my heart, with the stealthy pace of the tiger! I alternately laughed and howled, as the one or the other idea grew predominant.

Down—certainly, relentlessly down! It vibrated within three inches of my bosom! I struggled violently—furiously—to free my left arm. This was free only from the elbow to the hand. I could reach the latter, from the platter beside me, to my mouth, with great effort, but no farther. Could I have broken the fastenings above the elbow, I would have seized and attempted to arrest the pendulum. I might as well have attempted to arrest an avalanche!

Down — still unceasingly — still inevitably down! I gasped and struggled at each vibration. I shrunk convulsively at its every sweep. My eyes followed its outward or upward whorls with the eagerness of the most unmeaning despair; they closed themselves spasmodically at the descent, although death would have been a relief, oh, how unspeakable! Still I quivered in every nerve to think how slight a sinking of the machinery would precipitate that keen, glistening axe upon my bosom. It was *hope* that prompted the nerve to quiver—the frame to shrink. It was *hope*—the hope that triumphs on the rack—that whispers to the death-condemned even in the dungeons of the Inquisition.

I saw that some ten or twelve vibrations would bring the steel in actual contact with my robe—and with this observation there suddenly came over my spirit all the keen, collected calmness of despair. For the first time during many hours—or perhaps days—I *thought*. It now occurred to me, that the bandage, or surcingle, which enveloped me, *was unique*. I was tied by no separate cord. The first stroke of the razor-like crescent athwart any portion of the band would so detach it that it might be unwound from my person by means of my left hand. But how fearful, in that case, the proximity of the steel! The result of the slightest struggle, how deadly! Was it likely, moreover, that the minions of the torturer had not foreseen and provided for this possibility? Was it probable that the bandage crossed my bosom in the track of the pendulum? Dreading to find my faint and, as it seemed, my last hope frustrated, I so far elevated my head as to obtain a distinct view of my breast. The surcingle enveloped my limbs and body close in all directions—*save in the path of the destroying crescent.*

Scarcely had I dropped my head back into its original position, when there flashed upon my mind what I cannot better describe than as the unformed half of that idea of deliverance to which I have previously alluded, and of which a moiety only floated indeterminately through my brain when I raised food to my burning lips. The whole thought was now present—feeble, scarcely sane, scarcely definite—but still entire. I proceeded at once, with the nervous energy of despair, to attempt its execution.

For many hours the immediate vicinity of the low framework upon which I lay had been literally swarming with rats. They were wild, bold, ravenous—their red eyes glaring upon me as if they waited but for motionlessness on my part to make me their prey. " To what food," I thought, " have they been accustomed in the well ? "

They had devoured, in spite of all my efforts to prevent them, all but a small remnant of the contents of the dish. I had fallen into an habitual see-saw or wave of the hand about the platter; and, at length, the unconscious uniformity of the movement deprived it of effect. In their voracity, the vermin frequently fastened their sharp fangs in my fingers. With the particles of the oily and spicy viand which now remained, I thoroughly rubbed the bandage wherever I could reach it; then, raising my hand from the floor, I lay breathlessly still.

At first, the ravenous animals were startled and terrified at the change—at the cessation of movement. They shrank alarmedly back; many sought the well. But this was only for a moment. I had not counted in vain upon their voracity. Observing that I remained without motion, one or two of the boldest leaped upon the framework, and smelt at the surcingle. This seemed the signal for a general rush. Forth from the well they hurried in fresh troops. They clung to the wood—they overran it, and leaped in hundreds upon my person. The measured movement of the pendulum disturbed them not at all. Avoiding its strokes, they busied themselves with the anointed bandage. They pressed—they swarmed upon me in ever accumulating heaps. They writhed upon my throat; their cold lips sought my own; I was half stifled by their thronging pressure; disgust, for which the world has no name, swelled my bosom, and chilled, with a heavy clamminess, my heart. Yet one minute, and I felt that the struggle would be over. Plainly I perceived the loosening of the bandage. I knew that in more than one place it must be already severed. With a more than human resolution I lay *still*.

Nor had I erred in my calculations—nor had I endured in vain. I at length felt that I was *free*. The surcingle hung in ribands from my body. But the stroke of the pendulum already pressed upon my bosom. It had divided the serge of the robe. It had cut through the linen beneath. Twice again it swung, and a sharp sense of pain shot through every nerve. But the moment of escape had arrived. At a wave of my hand my deliverers hurried tumultuously away. With a steady movement—cautious, side-long, shrinking, and slow—I slid from the embrace of the bandage and beyond the reach of the scimitar. For the moment, at least, *I was free*.

Free!—and in the grasp of the Inquisition! I had scarcely stepped from my wooden bed of horror upon the stone floor of the prison, when the motion of the hellish machine ceased, and I beheld it drawn up, by some invisible force, through the ceiling. This was a lesson which I took desperately to heart. My every motion was undoubtedly watched. Free!—I had but escaped death in one form of agony, to be delivered unto worse than death in some other. With that thought I rolled my eyes nervously around on the barriers of iron that hemmed me in. Something unusual—some change which, at first, I could not appreciate distinctly—it was obvious, had taken place in the apartment. For many minutes of a dreamy and trembling abstraction, I busied myself in vain, unconnected conjecture. During this period, I became aware, for the first time, of the origin of the sulphurous light which illumined the cell. It proceeded from a fissure, about half an inch in width, extending entirely around the prison at the base of the walls, which thus appeared, and were completely separated from the floor. I endeavored, but of course in vain, to look through the aperture.

As I rose from the attempt, the mystery of the alteration in the chamber broke at once upon my understanding. I have observed that, although the outlines of the figures upon the walls were sufficiently distinct, yet the colors seemed blurred and indefinite. These colors had now assumed, and were momentarily assuming, a startling and most intense brilliancy, that gave to the spectral and fiendish portraitures an aspect that might have thrilled even firmer nerves than my own. Demon eyes, of a wild and ghastly vivacity, glared upon me in a thousand directions, where none had been visible before, and gleamed with the lurid lustre of a fire that I could not force my imagination to regard as unreal.

Unreal!—even while I breathed there came to my nostrils the breath of the vapor of heated iron! A suffocating odor pervaded the prison! A deeper glow settled each moment in the eyes that glared at my agonies! A richer tint of crimson diffused itself over the pictured horrors of blood. I panted! I gasped for breath! There could be no doubt of the design of my tormentors —oh! most unrelenting! oh! most demoniac of men! I shrank from the glowing metal to the centre of the cell. Amid the thought of the fiery destruction that impended, the idea of the coolness of the well came over my soul like balm. I rushed to its deadly brink. I threw my straining vision below. The glare from the enkindled roof illumined its inmost recesses. Yet, for a wild moment, did my spirit refuse to comprehend the meaning of what I saw. At length it forced —it wrestled its way into my soul—it burned itself in upon my shuddering reason. Oh! for a voice to speak!—oh! horror!—oh! any horror but this! With a shriek, I rushed from the margin, and buried my face in my hands—weeping bitterly.

The heat rapidly increased, and once again I looked up, shuddering as with a fit of the ague. There had been a second change in the cell— and now the change was obviously in the *form*. As before, it was in vain that I at first endeavored to appreciate or understand what was taking place. But not long was I left in doubt. The Inquisitorial vengeance had been hurried by my two-fold escape, and there was to be no more dallying with the King of Terrors. The room had been square. I saw that two of its iron angles were now acute—two, consequently, obtuse. The fearful difference quickly increased with a low rumbling or moaning sound. In an instant the apartment had shifted its form into that of a lozenge. But the alteration stopped not here—I neither hoped nor desired it to stop. I could have clasped the red walls to my bosom as a garment of eternal peace. "Death," I said, "any death but that of the pit!" Fool! might I not have known that *into the pit* it was the object of the burning iron to urge me? Could I resist its glow? or if even that, could I withstand its pressure? And now, flatter and flatter grew the lozenge, with a rapidity that left me no time for contemplation. Its centre, and of course its greatest width, came just over the yawning gulf. I shrank back—but the closing walls pressed me resistlessly onward. At length for my seared and writhing body there was no longer an inch of foothold on the firm floor of the prison. I struggled no more, but the agony of my soul found vent in one loud, long, and final scream of despair. I felt that I tottered upon the brink—I averted my eyes—

There was a discordant hum of human voices! There was a loud blast as of many trumpets! There was a harsh grating as of a thousand thunders! The fiery walls rushed back! An outstretched arm caught my own as I fell, fainting, into the abyss. It was that of General Lasalle. The French army had entered Toledo. The Inquisition was in the hands of its enemies.

THE PREMATURE BURIAL

[Published in unknown Philadelphia periodical, August, 1844. Later, in the *Broadway Journal*, I., 24.]

THERE are certain themes of which the interest is all-absorbing, but which are too entirely horrible for the purposes of legitimate fiction. These the mere romanticist must eschew, if he do not wish to offend, or to disgust. They are with propriety handled only when the severity and majesty of truth sanctify and sustain them. We thrill, for example, with the most intense of "pleasurable pain" over the accounts of the Passage of the Beresina, of the Earthquake at Lisbon, of the Plague at London, of the Massacre of St. Bartholomew, or of the stifling of the hundred and twenty-three prisoners in the Black Hole at Calcutta. But, in these accounts, it is the fact—it is the reality—it is the history which excites. As inventions, we should regard them with simple abhorrence.

I have mentioned some few of the more prominent and august calamities on record; but in these it is the extent, not less than the character of the calamity, which so vividly impresses the fancy. I need not remind the reader that, from the long and weird catalogue of human miseries, I might have selected many individual instances more replete with essential suffering than any of these vast generalities of disaster. The true wretchedness, indeed,—the ultimate woe,—is particular, not diffuse. That the ghastly extremes of agony are endured by man the unit, and never by man the mass—for this let us thank a merciful God!

To be buried while alive is, beyond question, the most terrific of these extremes which has ever fallen to the lot of mere mortality. That it has frequently, very frequently, so fallen will scarcely be denied by those who think. The boundaries which divide Life from Death are at best shadowy and vague. Who shall say where the one ends, and where the other begins? We know that there are diseases in which occur total cessations of all the apparent functions of vitality, and yet in which these cessations are merely suspensions, properly so called. They are only temporary pauses in the incomprehensible mechanism. A certain period elapses, and some unseen mysterious principle again sets in motion the magic pinions and the wizard wheels. The silver cord was not for ever loosed, nor the golden bowl irreparably broken. But where, meantime, was the soul?

Apart, however, from the inevitable conclusion, *a priori* that such causes must produce such effects,—that the well-known occurrence of such cases of suspended animation must naturally give rise, now and then, to premature interments,—apart from this consideration, we have the direct testimony of medical and ordinary experience to prove that a vast number of such interments have actually taken place. I might refer at once, if necessary, to a hundred well-authenticated instances. One of very remarkable character, and of which the circumstances may be fresh in the memory of some of my readers, occurred, not very long ago, in the neighboring city of Baltimore, where it occasioned a painful, intense, and widely-extended excitement. The wife of one of the most respectable citizens—a lawyer of eminence and a member of Congress—was seized with a sudden and unaccountable illness, which completely baffled the skill of her physicians. After much suffering she died, or was supposed to die. No one suspected, indeed, or had reason to suspect, that she was not actually dead. She presented all the ordinary appearances of death. The face assumed the usual pinched and sunken outline. The lips were of the usual marble pallor. The eyes were lustreless. There was no warmth. Pulsation had ceased. For three days the body was preserved unburied, during which it had acquired a stony rigidity. The funeral, in short, was hastened, on account of the rapid advance of what was supposed to be decomposition.

The lady was deposited in her family vault, which, for three subsequent years, was undisturbed. At the expiration of this term it was opened for the reception of a sarcophagus;—but, alas! how fearful a shock awaited the husband, who, personally, threw open the door! As its portals swung outwardly back, some white-apparelled object fell rattling within his arms. It was the skeleton of his wife in her yet unmoulded shroud.

A careful investigation rendered it evident that she had revived within two days after her entombment; that her struggles within the coffin had caused it to fall from a ledge, or shelf to the floor, where it was so broken as to permit her escape. A lamp which had been accidentally left, full of oil, within the tomb, was found empty; it might have been exhausted, however, by evaporation. On the uppermost of the steps which led down into the dread chamber was a large fragment of the coffin, with which it seemed that she had endeavored to arrest attention by striking the iron door. While thus occupied, she probably swooned, or possibly died, through sheer terror; and, in falling, her shroud became entangled in some iron-work which projected interiorly. Thus she remained, and thus she rotted, erect.

In the year 1810, a case of living inhumation happened in France, attended with circumstances which go far to warrant the assertion that truth is, indeed, stranger than fiction. The heroine of the story was a Mademoiselle Victorine Lafourcade, a young girl of illustrious family, of wealth, and of great personal beauty. Among her numerous suitors was Julien Bossuet, a poor *littérateur*, or journalist of Paris. His talents and general amiability had recommended him to the notice of the heiress, by whom he seems to have been truly beloved; but her pride of birth decided her, finally, to reject him, and to wed a Monsieur Renelle, a banker and a diplomatist of some eminence. After marriage, however, this gentleman neglected, and, perhaps, even more positively ill-treated her. Having passed with him some wretched years, she died—at least her condition so closely resembled death as to deceive every one who saw her. She was buried—not in a vault, but in an ordinary grave in the village of her nativity. Filled with despair, and still inflamed by the memory of a profound attachment, the lover journeys from the capital to the remote province in which the village lies, with the romantic purpose of disinterring the corpse, and possessing himself of its luxuriant tresses. He reaches the grave. At midnight he unearths the coffin, opens it, and is in the act of detaching the hair, when he is arrested by the unclosing of the beloved eyes. In fact, the lady had been buried alive. Vitality had not altogether departed, and she was aroused by the caresses of her lover from the lethargy which had been mistaken for death. He bore her frantically to his lodgings in the village. He employed certain powerful restoratives suggested by no little medical learning. In fine, she revived. She recognized her preserver. She remained with him until, by slow degrees, she fully recovered her original health. Her woman's heart was not adamant, and this last lesson of love sufficed to soften it. She bestowed it upon Bossuet. She returned no more to her husband, but, concealing from him her resurrection, fled with her lover to America. Twenty years afterward, the two returned to France, in the persuasion that time had so greatly altered the lady's appearance that her friends would be unable to recognize her. They were mistaken, however; for, at the first meeting, Monsieur Renelle did actually recognize and make claim to his wife. This claim she resisted, and a judicial tribunal sustained her in her resistance, deciding that the peculiar circumstances, with the long lapse of years, had extinguished, not only equitably, but legally, the authority of the husband.

The *Chirurgical Journal* of Leipsic, a periodical of high authority and merit, which some American book-seller would do well to translate and republish, records in a late number a very distressing event of the character in question.

An officer of artillery, a man of gigantic stature and of robust health, being thrown from an unmanageable horse, received a very severe contusion upon the head, which rendered him insensible at once; the skull was slightly fractured, but no immediate danger was apprehended. Trepanning was accomplished successfully. He was bled, and many other of the ordinary means of relief were adopted. Gradually, however, he fell into a more and more hopeless state of stupor, and, finally, it was thought that he died.

The weather was warm, and he was buried

with indecent haste in one of the public cemeteries. His funeral took place on Thursday. On the Sunday following, the grounds of the cemetery were, as usual, much thronged with visitors, and about noon an intense excitement was created by the declaration of a peasant that, while sitting upon the grave of the officer, he had distinctly felt a commotion of the earth, as if occasioned by some one struggling beneath. At first little attention was paid to the man's asseveration; but his evident terror, and the dogged obstinacy with which he persisted in his story, had at length their natural effect upon the crowd. Spades were hurriedly procured, and the grave, which was shamefully shallow, was in a few minutes so far thrown open that the head of its occupant appeared. He was then seemingly dead; but he sat nearly erect within his coffin, the lid of which, in his furious struggles, he had partially uplifted.

He was forthwith conveyed to the nearest hospital, and there pronounced to be still living, although in an asphytic condition. After some hours he revived, recognized individuals of his acquaintance, and, in broken sentences spoke of his agonies in the grave.

From what he related, it was clear that he must have been conscious of life for more than an hour, while inhumed, before lapsing into insensibility. The grave was carelessly and loosely filled with an exceedingly porous soil; and thus some air was necessarily admitted. He heard the footsteps of the crowd overhead, and endeavored to make himself heard in turn. It was the tumult within the grounds of the cemetery, he said, which appeared to awaken him from a deep sleep, but no sooner was he awake than he became fully aware of the awful horrors of his position.

This patient, it is recorded, was doing well, and seemed to be in a fair way of ultimate recovery, but fell a victim to the quackeries of medical experiment. The galvanic battery was applied, and he suddenly expired in one of those ecstatic paroxysms which, occasionally, it superinduces.

The mention of the galvanic battery, nevertheless, recalls to my memory a well-known and very extraordinary case in point, where its action proved the means of restoring to animation a young attorney of London, who had been interred for two days. This occurred in 1831, and created, at the time, a very profound sensation wherever it was made the subject of converse.

The patient, Mr. Edward Stapleton, had died, apparently, of typhus fever, accompanied with some anomalous symptoms which had excited the curiosity of his medical attendants. Upon his seeming decease, his friends were requested to sanction a *post-mortem* examination, but declined to permit it. As often happens, when such refusals are made, the practitioners resolved to disinter the body and dissect it at leisure, in private. Arrangements were easily effected with some of the numerous corps of body-snatchers with which London abounds; and, upon the third night after the funeral, the supposed corpse was unearthed from a grave eight feet deep, and deposited in the operating chamber of one of the private hospitals.

An incision of some extent had been actually made in the abdomen, when the fresh and undecayed appearance of the subject suggested an application of the battery. One experiment succeeded another, and the customary effects supervened, with nothing to characterize them in any respect, except, upon one or two occasions, a more than ordinary degree of life-likeness in the convulsive action.

It grew late. The day was about to dawn; and it was thought expedient, at length, to proceed at once to the dissection. A student, however, was especially desirous of testing a theory of his own, and insisted upon applying the battery to one of the pectoral muscles. A rough gash was made, and a wire hastily brought in contact; when the patient, with a hurried but quite unconvulsive movement, arose from the table, stepped into the middle of the floor, gazed about him uneasily for a few seconds, and then—spoke. What he said was unintelligible; but words were uttered; the syllabification was distinct. Having spoken, he fell heavily to the floor.

For some moments all were paralyzed with awe—but the urgency of the case soon restored them their presence of mind. It was seen that Mr. Stapleton was alive, although in a swoon. Upon exhibition of ether he revived and was rapidly restored to health, and to the society of his friends—from whom, however, all knowledge of his resuscitation was withheld, until a relapse was no longer to be apprehended. Their wonder—their rapturous astonishment—may be conceived.

The most thrilling peculiarity of this incident, nevertheless, is involved in what Mr. S. himself asserts. He declares that at no period was he altogether insensible—that, dully and confusedly, he was aware of everything which happened to him, from the moment in which he was pronounced *dead* by his physicians, to that in which he fell swooning to the floor of the hospital. "I am alive," were the uncomprehended words which, upon recognizing the locality of the dissecting-room, he had endeavored, in his extremity, to utter.

It were an easy matter to multiply such histories as these—but I forbear—for, indeed, we have no need of such to establish the fact that premature interments occur. When we reflect how very rarely, from the nature of the case, we have it in our power to detect them, we must admit that they may *frequently* occur without our cognizance. Scarcely, in truth, is a graveyard ever encroached upon, for any purpose, to any great extent, that skeletons are not found in postures which suggest the most fearful of suspicions.

Fearful indeed the suspicion—but more fearful the doom! It may be asserted, without hesitation, that *no* event is so terribly well adapted to inspire the supremeness of bodily and of mental distress, as is burial before death. The unendurable oppression of the lungs—the stifling fumes of the damp earth—the clinging to the death garments—the rigid embrace of the narrow house—the blackness of the absolute Night—the silence like a sea that overwhelms—the unseen but palpable presence of the Conqueror Worm—these things, with the thoughts of the air and grass above, with memory of dear friends who would fly to save us if but informed of our fate, and with consciousness that of this fate they can *never* be informed—that our hopeless portion is that of the really dead—these considerations, I say, carry into the heart, which still palpitates, a degree of appalling and intolerable horror from which the most daring imagination must recoil. We know of nothing so agonizing upon Earth—we can dream of nothing half so hideous in the realms of the nethermost Hell. And thus all narratives upon this topic have an interest profound; an interest, nevertheless, which, through the sacred awe of the topic itself, very properly and very peculiarly depends upon our conviction of the *truth* of the matter narrated. What I have now to tell is of my own actual knowledge—of my own positive and personal experience.

For several years I had been subject to attacks of the singular disorder which physicians have agreed to term catalepsy, in default of a more definite title. Although both the immediate and the predisposing causes, and even the actual diagnosis, of this disease are still mysterious, its obvious and apparent character is sufficiently well understood. Its variations seem to be chiefly of degree. Sometimes the patient lies, for a day only, or even for a shorter period, in a species of exaggerated lethargy. He is senseless and externally motionless; but the pulsation of the heart is still faintly perceptible; some traces of warmth remain; a slight color lingers within the centre of the cheek; and, upon application of a mirror to the lips, we can detect a torpid, unequal, and vacillating action of the lungs. Then again the duration of the trance is for weeks—even for months; while the closest scrutiny, and the most rigorous medical tests, fail to establish any material distinction between the state of the sufferer and what we conceive of absolute death. Very usually he is saved from premature interment solely by the knowledge of his friends that he has been previously subject to catalepsy, by the consequent suspicion excited, and, above all, by the non-appearance of decay. The advances of the malady are, luckily, gradual. The first manifestations, although marked, are unequivocal. The fits grow successively more and more distinctive, and endure each for a longer term than the preceding. In this lies the principal security from inhumation. The unfortunate whose *first* attack should be of the extreme character which is occasionally seen, would almost inevitably be consigned alive to the tomb.

My own case differed in no important particular from those mentioned in medical books.

Sometimes, without any apparent cause, I sank, little by little, into a condition of semi-syncope, or half swoon; and, in this condition, without pain, without ability to stir, or, strictly speaking, to think, but with a dull lethargic consciousness of life and of the presence of those who surrounded my bed, I remained, until the crisis of the disease restored me, suddenly, to perfect sensation. At other times I was quickly and impetuously smitten. I grew sick, and numb, and chilly, and dizzy, and so fell prostrate at once. Then, for weeks, all was void, and black, and silent, and Nothing became the universe. Total annihilation could be no more. From these latter attacks I awoke, however, with a gradation slow in proportion to the suddenness of the seizure. Just as the day dawns to the friendless and houseless beggar who roams the streets throughout the long desolate winter night—just so tardily—just so wearily—just so cheerily came back the light of the Soul to me.

Apart from the tendency to trance, however, my general health appeared to be good; nor could I perceive that it was at all affected by the one prevalent malady—unless, indeed, an idiosyncrasy in my ordinary *sleep* may be looked upon as superinduced. Upon awaking from slumber, I could never gain, at once, thorough possession of my senses, and always remained, for many minutes, in much bewilderment and perplexity—the mental faculties in general, but the memory in especial, being in a condition of absolute abeyance.

In all that I endured there was no physical suffering, but of moral distress an infinitude. My fancy grew charnel. I talked "of worms, of tombs, and epitaphs." I was lost in reveries of death, and the idea of premature burial held continual possession of my brain. The ghastly Danger to which I was subjected haunted me day and night. In the former, the torture of meditation was excessive; in the latter, supreme. When the grim Darkness overspread the Earth, then, with every horror of thought, I shook—shook as the quivering plumes upon the hearse. When Nature could endure wakefulness no longer, it was with a struggle that I consented to sleep—for I shuddered to reflect that, upon awaking, I might find myself the tenant of a grave. And when, finally, I sank into slumber, it was only to rush at once into a world of phantasms, above which, with vast, sable overshadowing wings, hovered, predominant, the one sepulchral Idea.

From the innumerable images of gloom which thus oppressed me in dreams, I select for record but a solitary vision. Methought I was immersed in a cataleptic trance of more than usual duration and profundity. Suddenly there came an icy hand upon my forehead, and an impatient, gibbering voice whispered the word "Arise!" within my ear.

I sat erect. The darkness was total. I could not see the figure of him who had aroused me. I could call to mind neither the period at which I had fallen into the trance, nor the locality in which I then lay. While I remained motionless, and busied in endeavors to collect my thought, the cold hand grasped me fiercely by the wrist, shaking it petulantly, while the gibbering voice said again:

"Arise! did I not bid thee arise?"

"And who," I demanded, "art thou?"

"I have no name in the regions which I inhabit," replied the voice, mournfully; "I was mortal, but am fiend. I was merciless, but am pitiful. Thou dost feel that I shudder. My teeth chatter as I speak, yet it is not with the chilliness of the night—of the night without end. But this hideousness is insufferable. How canst *thou* tranquilly sleep? I cannot rest for the cry of these great agonies. These sights are more than I can bear. Get thee up! Come with me into the outer Night, and let me unfold to thee the graves. Is not this a spectacle of woe?—Behold!"

I looked; and the unseen figure, which still grasped me by the wrist, had caused to be thrown open the graves of all mankind; and from each issued the faint phosphoric radiance of decay; so that I could see into the innermost recesses, and there view the shrouded bodies in their sad and solemn slumbers with the worm. But alas! the real sleepers were fewer, by many millions, than those who slumbered not at all; and there was a feeble struggling; and there was a general and sad unrest; and from out the depths of the countless pits there came a melancholy rustling from the garments of the buried. And of those who seemed tranquilly to repose, I saw that a vast number had changed, in a greater or less degree, the rigid and uneasy position in which they had originally been entombed. And the voice again said to me as I gazed:

"Is it not—oh! is it *not* a pitiful sight?" But before I could find words to reply, the figure had ceased to grasp my wrist, the phosphoric lights expired, and the graves were closed with a sudden violence, while from out them arose a tumult of despairing cries, saying again: "Is it not—Oh, God, is it *not* a very pitiful sight?"

Phantasies such as these, presenting themselves at night, extended their terrific influence far into my waking hours. My nerves became thoroughly unstrung, and I fell a prey to perpetual horror. I hesitated to ride, or to walk, or to indulge in any exercise that would carry me from home. In fact, I no longer dared trust myself out of the immediate presence of those who were aware of my proneness to catalepsy, lest, falling into one of my usual fits, I should be buried before my real condition could be ascertained. I doubted the care, the fidelity of my dearest friends. I dreaded that, in some trance of more than customary duration, they might be prevailed upon to regard me as irrecoverable. I even went so far as to fear that, as I occasioned much trouble, they might be glad to consider any very protracted attack as sufficient excuse for getting rid of me altogether. It was in vain they endeavored to reassure me by the most solemn promises. I exacted the most sacred oaths, that under no circumstances they would bury me until decomposition had so materially advanced as to render further preservation impossible. And, even then, my mortal terrors would listen to no reason—would accept no consolation. I entered into a series of elaborate precautions. Among other things, I had the family vault so remodelled as to admit of being readily opened from within. The slightest pressure upon a long lever that extended far into the tomb would cause the iron portals to fly back. There were arrangements also for the free admission of air and light, and convenient receptacles for food and water, within immediate reach of the coffin intended for my reception. This coffin was warmly and softly padded, and was provided with a lid, fashioned upon the principle of the vault-door, with the addition of springs so contrived that the feeblest movement of the body would be sufficient to set it at liberty. Besides all this, there was suspended from the roof of the tomb, a large bell, the rope of which, it was designed, should extend through a hole in the coffin, and so be fastened to one of the hands of the corpse. But, alas! what avails the vigilance against the Destiny of man? Not even these well-contrived securities sufficed to save from the uttermost agonies of living inhumation, a wretch to these agonies foredoomed!

There arrived an epoch—as often before there had arrived—in which I found myself emerging from total unconsciousness into the first feeble and indefinite sense of existence. Slowly—with a tortoise gradation—approached the faint gray dawn of the psychal day. A torpid uneasiness.

An apathetic endurance of dull pain. No care—no hope—no effort. Then, after a long interval, a ringing in the ears; then, after a lapse still longer, a prickling or tingling sensation in the extremities; then a seemingly eternal period of pleasurable quiescence, during which the awakening feelings are struggling into thought; then a brief re-sinking into nonentity; then a sudden recovery. At length the slight quivering of an eyelid, and immediately thereupon, an electric shock of a terror, deadly and indefinite, which sends the blood in torrents from the temples to the heart. And now the first positive effort to think. And now the first endeavor to remember. And now a partial and evanescent success. And now the memory has so far regained its dominion, that, in some measure, I am cognizant of my state. I feel that I am not awaking from ordinary sleep. I recollect that I have been subject to catalepsy. And now, at last, as if by the rush of an ocean, my shuddering spirit is overwhelmed by the one grim Danger—by the one spectral and ever-prevalent Idea.

For some minutes after this fancy possessed me, I remained without motion. And why? I could not summon courage to move. I dared not make the effort which was to satisfy me of my fate—and yet there was something at my heart which whispered me *it was sure.* Despair—such as no other species of wretchedness ever calls into being—despair alone urged me, after long irresolution, to uplift the heavy lids of my eyes. I uplifted them. It was dark—all dark. I knew that the fit was over. I knew that the crisis of my disorder had long passed. I knew that I had now fully recovered the use of my visual faculties—and yet it was dark—all dark—the intense and utter raylessness of the Night that endureth for evermore.

I endeavored to shriek; and my lips and my parched tongue moved convulsively together in the attempt—but no voice issued from the cavernous lungs, which, oppressed as if by the weight of some incumbent mountain, gasped and palpitated, with the heart, at every elaborate and struggling inspiration.

The movement of the jaws, in this effort to cry aloud, showed me that they were bound up, as is usual with the dead. I felt, too, that I lay upon some hard substance; and by something similar my sides were, also, closely compressed. So far, I had not ventured to stir any of my limbs—but now I violently threw up my arms, which had been lying at length, with the wrists crossed. They struck a solid wooden substance, which extended above my person at an elevation of not more than six inches from my face. I could no longer doubt that I reposed within a coffin at last.

And now, amid all my infinite miseries, came sweetly the cherub Hope—for I thought of my precautions. I writhed, and made spasmodic exertions to force open the lid: it would not move. I felt my wrists for the bell-rope: it was not to be found. And now the Comforter fled for ever, and a still sterner Despair reigned triumphant;

for I could not help perceiving the absence of the paddings which I had so carefully prepared—and then, too, there came suddenly to my nostrils the strong peculiar odor of moist earth. The conclusion was irresistible. I was *not* within the vault. I had fallen into a trance while absent from home—while among strangers—when, or how, I could not remember—and it was they who had buried me as a dog—nailed up in some common coffin—and thrust deep, deep, and for ever, into some ordinary and nameless *grave.*

As this awful conviction forced itself, thus, into the innermost chambers of my soul, I once again struggled to cry aloud. And in this second endeavor I succeeded. A long, wild, and continuous shriek, or yell, of agony, resounded through the realms of the subterranean Night.

"Hillo! hillo, there!" said a gruff voice, in reply.

"What the devil's the matter now!" said a second.

"Get out o' that!" said a third.

"What do you mean by yowling in that ere kind of style, like a catymount?" said a fourth; and hereupon I was seized and shaken without ceremony, for several minutes, by a junto of very rough-looking individuals. They did not arouse me from my slumber—for I was wide-awake when I screamed—but they restored me to the full possession of my memory.

This adventure occurred near Richmond, in Virginia. Accompanied by a friend, I had proceeded, upon a gunning expedition, some miles down the banks of the James River. Night approached, and we were overtaken by a storm. The cabin of a small sloop lying at anchor in the stream, and laden with garden mould, afforded us the only available shelter. We made the best of it, and passed the night on board. I slept in one of the only two berths in the vessel—and the berths of a sloop of sixty or seventy tons need scarcely be described. That which I occupied had no bedding of any kind. Its extreme width was eighteen inches. The distance of its bottom from the deck overhead was precisely the same. I found it a matter of exceeding difficulty to squeeze myself in. Nevertheless, I slept soundly; and the whole of my vision—for it was no dream, and no nightmare—arose naturally from the circumstances of my position—from my ordinary bias of thought—and from the difficulty, to which I have alluded, of collecting my senses, and especially of regaining my memory, for a long time after awaking from slumber. The men who shook me were the crew of the sloop, and some laborers engaged to unload it. From the load itself came the earthy smell. The bandage about the jaws was a silk handkerchief in which I had bound up my head, in default of my customary nightcap.

The tortures endured, however, were indubitably quite equal, for the time, to those of actual sepulture. They were fearfully—they were inconceivably hideous; but out of Evil proceeded Good; for their very excess wrought in my spirit an inevitable revulsion. My soul acquired tone

—acquired temper. I went abroad. I took vigorous exercise. I breathed the free air of Heaven. I thought upon other subjects than Death. I discarded my medical books. "Buchan" I burned. I read no "Night Thoughts"—no fustian about church-yards—no bugaboo tales—*such as this.* In short I became a new man, and lived a man's life. From that memorable night, I dismissed forever my charnel apprehensions, and with them vanished the cataleptic disorder, of which, perhaps, they had been less the consequence than the cause.

There are moments when, even to the sober eye of Reason, the world of our sad Humanity may assume the semblance of a Hell—but the imagination of man is no Carathis, to explore with impunity its every cavern. Alas! the grim legion of sepulchral terrors cannot be regarded as altogether fanciful—but, like the Demons in whose company Afrasiab made his voyage down the Oxus, they must sleep, or they will devour us—they must be suffered to slumber, or we perish.

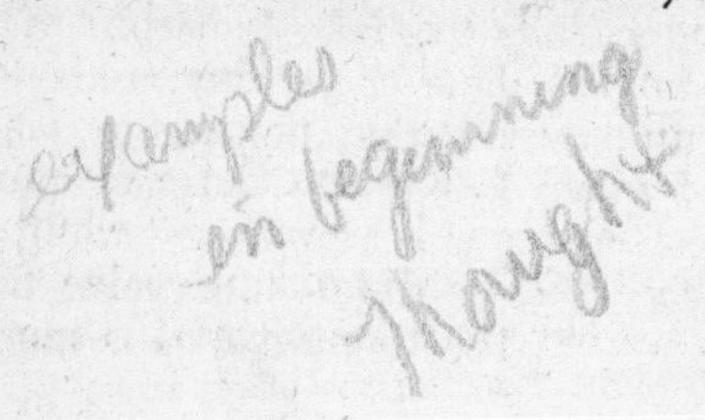

THE CASK OF AMONTILLADO

[Published in *Godey's Lady's Book,* November, 1846.]

THE thousand injuries of Fortunato I had borne as I best could; but when he ventured upon insult, I vowed revenge. You, who so well know the nature of my soul, will not suppose, however, that I gave utterance to a threat. *At length* I would be avenged; this was a point definitely settled—but the very definitiveness with which it was resolved, precluded the idea of risk. I must not only punish, but punish with impunity. A wrong is unredressed when retribution overtakes its redresser. It is equally unredressed when the avenger fails to make himself felt as such to him who has done the wrong.

It must be understood, that neither by word nor deed had I given Fortunato cause to doubt my good-will. I continued, as was my wont, to smile in his face, and he did not perceive that my smile *now* was at the thought of his immolation.

He had a weak point—this Fortunato—although in other regards he was a man to be respected and even feared. He prided himself on his connoisseurship in wine. Few Italians have the true virtuoso spirit. For the most part their enthusiasm is adapted to suit the time and opportunity—to practise imposture upon the British and Austrian *millionaires*. In painting and gemmary Fortunato, like his countrymen, was a quack—but in the matter of old wines he was sincere. In this respect I did not differ from him materially: I was skilful in the Italian vintages myself, and bought largely whenever I could.

It was about dusk, one evening during the supreme madness of the carnival season, that I encountered my friend. He accosted me with excessive warmth, for he had been drinking much. The man wore motley. He had on a tight-fitting parti-striped dress, and his head was surmounted by the conical cap and bells. I was so pleased to see him, that I thought I should never have done wringing his hand.

I said to him: "My dear Fortunato, you are luckily met. How remarkably well you are looking to-day! But I have received a pipe of what passes for Amontillado, and I have my doubts."

"How?" said he. "Amontillado? A pipe? Impossible! And in the middle of the carnival!"

"I have my doubts," I replied; "and I was silly enough to pay the full Amontillado price without consulting you in the matter. You were not to be found, and I was fearful of losing a bargain."

"Amontillado!"

"I have my doubts."

"Amontillado!"

"And I must satisfy them."

"Amontillado!"

"As you are engaged, I am on my way to Luchesi. If any one has a critical turn, it is he. He will tell me——"

"Luchesi cannot tell Amontillado from Sherry."

"And yet some fools will have it that his taste is a match for your own."

"Come, let us go."

"Whither?"

"To your vaults."

"My friend, no; I will not impose upon your good nature. I perceive you have an engagement. Luchesi——"

"I have no engagement;—come."

"My friend, no. It is not the engagement, but the severe cold with which I perceive you are afflicted. The vaults are insufferably damp. They are encrusted with nitre."

"Let us go, nevertheless. The cold is merely nothing. Amontillado! You have been imposed upon. And as for Luchesi, he cannot distinguish Sherry from Amontillado."

Thus speaking, Fortunato possessed himself of my arm. Putting on a mask of black silk, and drawing a *roquelaire* closely about my person, I suffered him to hurry me to my palazzo.

There were no attendants at home; they had absconded to make merry in honor of the time. I had told them that I should not return until the morning, and had given them explicit orders not to stir from the house. These orders were sufficient, I well knew, to insure their immediate disappearance, one and all, as soon as my back was turned.

I took from their sconces two flambeaux, and giving one to Fortunato, bowed him through several suites of rooms to the archway that led into the vaults. I passed down a long and winding staircase, requesting him to be cautious as he followed. We came at length to the foot of the descent, and stood together on the damp ground of the catacombs of the Montresors.

The gait of my friend was unsteady, and the bells upon his cap jingled as he strode.

"The pipe?" said he.

"It is farther on," said I; "but observe the white webwork which gleams from these cavern walls."

He turned toward me, and looked into my eyes with two filmy orbs that distilled the rheum of intoxication.

"Nitre?" he asked, at length.

"Nitre," I replied. "How long have you had that cough?"

"Ugh! ugh! ugh!—ugh! ugh! ugh!—ugh! ugh! ugh!—ugh! ugh! ugh!—ugh! ugh! ugh!"

My poor friend found it impossible to reply for many minutes.

"It is nothing," he said, at last.

"Come," I said, with decision, "we will go back; your health is precious. You are rich, respected, admired, beloved; you are happy, as once I was. You are a man to be missed. For me it is no matter. We will go back; you will be ill, and I cannot be responsible. Besides, there is Luchesi——"

"Enough," he said; "the cough is a mere nothing; it will not kill me. I shall not die of a cough."

"True—true," I replied; "and, indeed, I had no intention of alarming you unnecessarily; but you should use all proper caution. A draught of this Medoc will defend us from the damps."

Here I knocked off the neck of a bottle which I drew from a long row of its fellows that lay upon the mould.

"Drink," I said, presenting him the wine.

He raised it to his lips with a leer. He paused and nodded to me familiarly, while his bells jingled.

"I drink," he said, "to the buried that repose around us."

"And I to your long life."

He again took my arm, and we proceeded.

"These vaults," he said, "are extensive."

"The Montresors," I replied, "were a great and numerous family."

"I forgot your arms."

"A huge human foot d'or, in a field azure; the foot crushes a serpent rampant whose fangs are imbedded in the heel."

"And the motto?"

"*Nemo me impune lacessit.*"

"Good!" he said.

The wine sparkled in his eyes and the bells jingled. My own fancy grew warm with the

Medoc. We had passed through walls of piled bones, with casks and puncheons intermingling, into the inmost recesses of the catacombs. I paused again, and this time I made bold to seize Fortunato by an arm above the elbow.

"The nitre!" I said; "see, it increases. It hangs like moss upon the vaults. We are below the river's bed. The drops of moisture trickle among the bones. Come, we will go back ere it is too late. Your cough——"

"It is nothing," he said; "let us go on. But first, another draught of the Medoc."

I broke and reached him a flagon of De Grâve. He emptied it at a breath. His eyes flashed with a fierce light. He laughed and threw the bottle upward with a gesticulation I did not understand.

I looked at him in surprise. He repeated the movement—a grotesque one.

"You do not comprehend?" he said.

"Not I," I replied.

"Then you are not of the brotherhood."

"How?"

"You are not of the masons."

"Yes, yes," I said; "yes, yes."

"You? Impossible! A mason?"

"A mason," I replied.

"A sign," he said.

"It is this," I answered, producing a trowel from beneath the folds of my *roquelaire*.

"You jest," he exclaimed, recoiling a few paces. "But let us proceed to the Amontillado."

"Be it so," I said, replacing the tool beneath

the cloak, and again offering him my arm. He leaned upon it heavily. We continued our route in search of the Amontillado. We passed through a range of low arches, descended, passed on, and descending again, arrived at a deep crypt, in which the foulness of the air caused our flambeaux rather to glow than flame.

At the most remote end of the crypt there appeared another less spacious. Its walls had been lined with human remains, piled to the vault overhead, in the fashion of the great catacombs of Paris. Three sides of this interior crypt were still ornamented in this manner. From the fourth the bones had been thrown down, and lay promiscuously upon the earth, forming at one point a mound of some size. Within the wall thus exposed by the displacing of the bones, we perceived a still interior recess, in depth about four feet, in width three, in height six or seven. It seemed to have been constructed for no especial use within itself, but formed merely the interval between two of the colossal supports of the roof of the catacombs, and was backed by one of their circumscribing walls of solid granite.

It was in vain that Fortunato, uplifting his dull torch, endeavored to pry into the depth of the recess. Its termination the feeble light did not enable us to see.

"Proceed," I said; "herein is the Amontillado. As for Luchesi——"

"He is an ignoramus," interrupted my friend, as he stepped unsteadily forward, while I followed immediately at his heels. In an instant he had reached the extremity of the niche, and finding his progress arrested by the rock, stood stupidly bewildered. A moment more and I had fettered him to the granite. In its surface were two iron staples, distant from each other about two feet, horizontally. From one of these depended a short chain, from the other a padlock. Throwing the links about his waist, it was but the work of a few seconds to secure it. He was too much astounded to resist. Withdrawing the key I stepped back from the recess.

"Pass your hand," I said, "over the wall; you cannot help feeling the nitre. Indeed it is *very* damp. Once more let me *implore* you to return. No? Then I must positively leave you. But I must first render you all the little attentions in my power."

"The Amontillado!" ejaculated my friend, not yet recovered from his astonishment.

"True," I replied; "the Amontillado."

As I said these words I busied myself among the pile of bones of which I have before spoken. Throwing them aside, I soon uncovered a quantity of building stone and mortar. With these materials and with the aid of my trowel, I began vigorously to wall up the entrance of the niche.

I had scarcely laid the first tier of the masonry when I discovered that the intoxication of Fortunato had in a great measure worn off. The earliest indication I had of this was a low moaning cry from the depth of the recess. It was *not* the cry of a drunken man. There was then a long and obstinate silence. I laid the second tier, and the third, and the fourth; and then I heard the furious vibrations of the chain. The noise lasted for several minutes, during which, that I might hearken to it with the more satisfaction, I ceased my labors and sat down upon the bones. When at last the clanking subsided, I resumed the trowel, and finished without interruption the fifth, the sixth, and the seventh tier. The wall was now nearly upon a level with my breast. I again paused, and holding the flambeaux over the mason-work, threw a few feeble rays upon the figure within.

A succession of loud and shrill screams, bursting suddenly from the throat of the chained form, seemed to thrust me violently back. For a brief moment I hesitated—I trembled. Unsheathing my rapier, I began to grope with it about the recess; but the thought of an instant reassured me. I placed my hand upon the solid fabric of the catacombs, and felt satisfied. I reapproached the wall. I replied to the yells of him who clamored. I re-echoed—I aided—I surpassed them in volume and in strength. I did this, and the clamorer grew still.

It was now midnight, and my task was drawing to a close. I had completed the eighth, the ninth, and the tenth tier. I had finished a portion of the last and the eleventh; there remained but a single stone to be fitted and plastered in. I struggled with its weight; I placed it partially in its destined position. But now there came from out the niche a low laugh that erected the hairs upon my head. It was succeeded by a sad voice, which I had difficulty in recognizing as that of the noble Fortunato. The voice said—

"Ha! ha! ha!—he! he!—a very good joke indeed—an excellent jest. We will have many a rich laugh about it at the palazzo—he! he! he!—over our wine—he! he! he!"

"The Amontillado!" I said.

"He! he! he!—he! he! he;—yes, the Amontillado. But is it not getting late? Will not they be awaiting us at the palazzo, the Lady Fortunato and the rest? Let us be gone."

"Yes," I said, "let us be gone."

"*For the love of God, Montresor!*"

"Yes," I said, "for the love of God!"

But to these words I hearkened in vain for a reply. I grew impatient. I called aloud:

"Fortunato!"

No answer. I called again:

"Fortunato!"

No answer still. I thrust a torch through the remaining aperture and let it fall within. There came forth in return only a jingling of the bells. My heart grew sick—on account of the dampness of the catacombs. I hastened to make an end of my labor. I forced the last stone into its position; I plastered it up. Against the new masonry I re-erected the old rampart of bones. For the half of a century no mortal has disturbed them. *In pace requiescat!*

THE TELL-TALE HEART

[Published in *The Pioneer*, January, 1843.]

TRUE!—nervous—very, very dreadfully nervous I had been and am! but why *will* you say that I am mad? The disease had sharpened my senses—not destroyed—not dulled them. Above all was the sense of hearing acute. I heard all things in the heaven and in the earth. I heard many things in hell. How, then, am I mad? Hearken! and observe how healthily—how calmly I can tell you the whole story.

It is impossible to say how first the idea entered my brain; but once conceived, it haunted me day and night. Object there was none. Passion there was none. I loved the old man. He had never wronged me. He had never given me insult. For his gold I had no desire. I think it was his eye! yes, it was this! One of his eyes resembled that of a vulture—a pale blue eye, with a film over it. Whenever it fell upon me, my blood ran cold; and so by degrees—very gradually—I made up my mind to take the life of the old man, and thus rid myself of the eye for ever.

Now this is the point. You fancy me mad. Madmen know nothing. But you should have seen *me*. You should have seen how wisely I proceeded—with what caution—with what foresight—with what dissimulation I went to work! I was never kinder to the old man than during the whole week before I killed him. And every night, about midnight, I turned the latch of his door and opened it—oh, so gently! And then, when I had made an opening sufficient for my head, I put in a dark lantern, all closed, closed, so that no light shone out, and then I thrust in my head. Oh, you would have laughed to see how cunningly I thrust it in! I moved it slowly—very, very slowly, so that I might not disturb the old man's sleep. It took me an hour to place my whole head within the opening so far that I could see him as he lay upon his bed. Ha!—would a madman have been so wise as this? And then, when my head was well in the room, I undid the lantern cautiously—oh, so cautiously—cautiously (for the hinges creaked)—I undid it just so much that a single thin ray fell upon the vulture eye. And this I did for seven long nights—every night just at midnight—but I found the eye always closed; and so it was impossible to do the work; for it was not the old man who vexed me, but his Evil Eye. And every morning, when the day broke, I went boldly into the chamber, and spoke courageously to him, calling him by name in a hearty tone, and inquiring how he had passed the night. So you see he would have been a very profound old man, indeed, to suspect that every night, just at twelve, I looked in upon him while he slept.

Upon the eighth night I was more than usually cautious in opening the door. A watch's minute hands moves more quickly than did mine. Never before that night had I *felt* the extent of my own powers—of my sagacity. I could scarcely contain my feelings of triumph. To think that there I was, opening the door, little by little, and he not even to dream of my secret deeds or thoughts. I fairly chuckled at the idea; and perhaps he heard me; for he moved on the bed suddenly, as if startled. Now you may think that I drew back—but no. His room was as black as pitch with the thick darkness, (for the shutters were close fastened, through fear of robbers,) and so I knew that he could not see the opening of the door, and I kept pushing it on steadily, steadily.

I had my head in, and was about to open the lantern, when my thumb slipped upon the tin fastening, and the old man sprang up in the bed, crying out—"Who's there?"

I kept quite still and said nothing. For a whole hour I did not move a muscle, and in the meantime I did not hear him lie down. He was still sitting up in the bed listening;—just as I have done, night after night, hearkening to the death watches in the wall.

Presently I heard a slight groan, and I knew it was the groan of mortal terror. It was not a groan of pain or of grief—oh no!—it was the low stifled sound that arises from the bottom of the soul when overcharged with awe. I knew the sound well. Many a night, just at midnight, when all the world slept, it has welled up from my own bosom, deepening, with its dreadful echo, the terrors that distracted me. I say I knew it well. I knew what the old man felt, and pitied him, although I chuckled at heart. I knew that he had been lying awake ever since the first slight noise, when he had turned in the bed. His fears had been ever since growing upon him. He had been trying to fancy them causeless, but could not. He had been saying to himself—"It is nothing but the wind in the chimney—it is only a mouse crossing the floor," or "it is merely a cricket which has made a single chirp." Yes, he has been trying to comfort himself with these suppositions; but he had found all in vain. *All in vain;* because Death, in approaching him, had stalked with his black shadow before him, and enveloped the victim. And it was the mournful influence of the unperceived shadow that caused him to feel —although he neither saw nor heard—to *feel* the presence of my head within the room.

When I had waited a long time, very patiently, without hearing him lie down, I resolved to open a little—a very, very little crevice in the lantern. So I opened it—you cannot imagine how stealthily, stealthily—until, at length, a single dim ray, like the thread of the spider, shot from out the crevice and full upon the vulture eye.

It was open—wide, wide open—and I grew

furious as I gazed upon it. I saw it with perfect distinctness—all a dull blue, with a hideous veil over it that chilled the very marrow in my bones; but I could see nothing else of the old man's face or person: for I had directed the ray as if by instinct, precisely upon the damned spot.

And now have I not told you that what you mistake for madness is but over-acuteness of the senses?—now, I say, there came to my ears a low, dull, quick sound, such as a watch makes when enveloped in cotton. I knew *that* sound well too. It was the beating of the old man's heart. It increased my fury, as the beating of a drum stimulates the soldier into courage.

But even yet I refrained and kept still. I scarcely breathed. I held the lantern motionless. I tried how steadily I could maintain the ray upon the eye. Meantime the hellish tattoo of the heart increased. It grew quicker and quicker, and louder and louder every instant. The old man's terror *must* have been extreme! It grew louder, I say, louder every moment!—do you mark me well? I have told you that I am nervous: so I am. And now at the dead hour of the night, amid the dreadful silence of that old house, so strange a noise as this excited me to uncontrollable terror. Yet, for some minutes longer I refrained and stood still. But the beating grew louder, louder! I thought the heart must burst. And now a new anxiety seized me—the sound would be heard by a neighbor! The old man's hour had come!

With a loud yell, I threw open the lantern and leaped into the room. He shrieked once—once only. In an instant I dragged him to the floor, and pulled the heavy bed over him. I then smiled gaily, to find the deed so far done. But, for many minutes, the heart beat on with a muffled sound. This, however, did not vex me; it would not be heard through the wall. At length it ceased. The old man was dead. I removed the bed and examined the corpse. Yes, he was stone, stone dead. I placed my hand upon the heart and held it there many minutes. There was no pulsation. He was stone dead. His eye would trouble me no more.

If still you think me mad, you will think so no longer when I describe the wise precautions I took for the concealment of the body. The night waned, and I worked hastily, but in silence. First of all I dismembered the corpse. I cut off the head and the arms and the legs.

I then took up three planks from the flooring of the chamber, and deposited all between the scantlings. I then replaced the boards so cleverly, so cunningly, that no human eye—not even *his*—could have detected any thing wrong. There was nothing to wash out—no stain of any kind—no blood-spot whatever. I had been too wary for that. A tub had caught all—ha! ha!

When I had made an end of these labors, it was four o'clock—still dark as midnight. As the bell sounded the hour, there came a knocking at the street door. I went down to open it with a light heart,—for what had I *now* to fear?

There entered three men, who introduced themselves, with perfect suavity, as officers of the police. A shriek had been heard by a neighbor during the night; suspicion of foul play had been aroused; information had been lodged at the police office, and they (the officers) had been deputed to search the premises.

I smiled,—for *what* had I to fear? I bade the gentlemen welcome. The shriek, I said, was my own in a dream. The old man, I mentioned, was absent in the country. I took my visitors all over the house. I bade them search—search *well.* I led them, at length, to *his* chamber. I showed them his treasures, secure, undisturbed. In the enthusiasm of my confidence, I brought chairs into the room, and desired them *here* to rest from their fatigues, while I myself, in the wild audacity of my perfect triumph, placed my own seat upon the very spot beneath which reposed the corpse of the victim.

The officers were satisfied. My *manner* had convinced them. I was singularly at ease. They sat, and while I answered cheerily, they chatted familiar things. But, ere long, I felt myself getting pale and wished them gone. My head ached, and I fancied a ringing in my ears: but still they sat and still chatted. The ringing became more distinct:—it continued and became more distinct: I talked more freely to get rid of the feeling: but it continued and gained definitiveness—until, at length, I found that the noise was *not* within my ears.

No doubt I now grew *very* pale;—but I

talked more fluently, and with a heightened voice. Yet the sound increased—and what could I do? It was *a low, dull, quick sound—much such a sound as a watch makes when enveloped in cotton.* I gasped for breath—and yet the officers heard it not. I talked more quickly—more vehemently; but the noise steadily increased. I arose and argued about trifles, in a high key and with violent gesticulations, but the noise steadily increased. Why *would* they not be gone? I paced the floor to and fro with heavy strides, as if excited to fury by the observation of the men—but the noise steadily increased. Oh God! what *could* I do? I foamed—I raved—I swore! I swung the chair upon which I had been sitting, and grated it upon the boards, but the noise arose over all and continually increased. It grew louder—louder—*louder!* And still the men chatted pleasantly, and smiled. Was it possible they heard not? Almighty God!—no, no! They heard!—they suspected!—they *knew!*—they were making a *mockery* of my horror!—this I thought, and this I think. But any thing was better than this agony! Any thing was more tolerable than this derision! I could bear those hypocritical smiles no longer! I felt that I must scream or die!—and now—again—hark! louder! louder! louder! *louder!*—

"Villains!" I shrieked, "dissemble no more! I admit the deed!—tear up the planks!—here, here!—it is the beating of his hideous heart!"

THE BLACK CAT

[Published in *The Philadelphia United States Saturday Post,* August 19, 1843.]

For the most wild yet most homely narrative which I am about to pen, I neither expect nor solicit belief. Mad indeed would I be to expect it, in a case where my very senses reject their own evidence. Yet, mad am I not—and very surely do I not dream. But to-morrow I die, and to-day I would unburden my soul. My immediate purpose is to place before the world, plainly, succinctly, and without comment, a series of mere household events. In their consequences, these events have terrified—have tortured—have destroyed me. Yet I will not attempt to expound them. To me, they have presented little but horror—to many they will seem less terrible than *baroques.* Hereafter, perhaps, some intellect may be found which will reduce my phantasm to the commonplace—some intellect more calm, more logical, and far less excitable than my own, which will perceive, in the circumstances I detail with awe, nothing more than an ordinary succession of very natural causes and effects.

From my infancy I was noted for the docility and humanity of my disposition. My tenderness of heart was even so conspicuous as to make me the jest of my companions. I was especially fond of animals, and was indulged by my parents with a great variety of pets. With these I spent most of my time, and never was so happy as when feeding and caressing them. This peculiarity of character grew with my growth, and, in my manhood, I derived from it one of my principal sources of pleasure. To those who have cherished an affection for a faithful and sagacious dog, I need hardly be at the trouble of explaining the nature or the intensity of the gratification thus derivable. There is something in the unselfish and self-sacrificing love of a brute, which goes directly to the heart of him who has had frequent occasion to test the paltry friendship and gossamer fidelity of mere *Man*.

I married early, and was happy to find in my wife a disposition not uncongenial with my own. Observing my partiality for domestic pets, she lost no opportunity of procuring those of the most agreeable kind. We had birds, gold-fish, a fine dog, rabbits, a small monkey, and a *cat*.

This latter was a remarkably large and beautiful animal, entirely black, and sagacious to an astonishing degree. In speaking of his intelligence, my wife, who at heart was not a little tinctured with superstition, made frequent allusion to the ancient popular notion, which regarded all black cats as witches in disguise. Not that she was ever *serious* upon this point—and I mention the matter at all for no better reason than that it happens, just now, to be remembered.

Pluto—this was the cat's name—was my favorite pet and playmate. I alone fed him, and he attended me wherever I went about the house. It was even with difficulty that I could prevent him from following me through the streets.

Our friendship lasted, in this manner, for several years, during which my general temperament and character—through the instrumentality of the Fiend Intemperance—had (I blush to confess it) experienced a radical alteration for the worse. I grew, day by day, more moody, more irritable, more regardless of the feelings of others. I suffered myself to use intemperate language to my wife. At length, I even offered her personal violence. My pets, of course, were made to feel the change in my disposition. I not only neglected, but ill-used them. For Pluto, however, I still retained sufficient regard to restrain me from maltreating him, as I made no scruple of maltreating the rabbits, the monkey, or even the dog, when, by accident, or through affection, they came in my way. But my disease grew upon me—for what disease is like Alcohol!—and at length even Pluto, who was now becoming old, and consequently somewhat peevish—even Pluto began to experience the effects of my ill temper.

One night, returning home, much intoxicated,

from one of my haunts about town, I fancied that the cat avoided my presence. I seized him; when, in his fright at my violence, he inflicted a slight wound upon my hand with his teeth. The fury of a demon instantly possessed me. I knew myself no longer. My original soul seemed, at once, to take its flight from my body; and a more than fiendish malevolence, gin-nurtured, thrilled every fibre of my frame. I took from my waistcoat-pocket a penknife, opened it, grasped the poor beast by the throat, and deliberately cut one of its eyes from the socket! I blush, I burn, I shudder, while I pen the damnable atrocity.

When reason returned with the morning—when I had slept off the fumes of the night's debauch—I experienced a sentiment half of horror, half of remorse, for the crime of which I had been guilty; but it was, at best, a feeble and equivocal feeling, and the soul remained untouched. I again plunged into excess, and soon drowned in wine all memory of the deed.

In the meantime the cat slowly recovered. The socket of the lost eye presented, it is true, a frightful appearance, but he no longer appeared to suffer any pain. He went about the house as usual, but, as might be expected, fled in extreme terror at my approach. I had so much of my old heart left, as to be at first grieved by this evident dislike on the part of a creature which had once so loved me. But this feeling soon gave place to irritation. And then came, as if to my final and irrevocable overthrow, the spirit of PERVERSE-

NESS.* Of this spirit philosophy takes no account. Yet I am not more sure that my soul lives, than I am that perverseness is one of the primitive impulses of the human heart—one of the indivisible primary faculties, or sentiments, which give direction to the character of Man. Who has not, a hundred times, found himself committing a vile or a stupid action, for no other reason than because he knows he should *not?* Have we not a perpetual inclination, in the teeth of our best judgment, to violate that which is *Law*, merely because we understand it to be such? This spirit of perverseness, I say, came to my final overthrow. It was this unfathomable longing of the soul *to vex itself*—to offer violence to its own nature—to do wrong for the wrong's sake only—that urged me to continue and finally to consummate the injury I had inflicted upon the unoffending brute. One morning, in cold blood, I slipped a noose about its neck and hung it to the limb of a tree;—hung it with the tears streaming from my eyes, and with the bitterest remorse at my heart;—hung it *because* I knew that it had loved me, and *because* I felt it had given me no reason of offence;—hung it *because* I knew that in so doing I was committing a sin—a deadly sin that would so jeopardize my immortal soul as to place it—if such a thing were possible—even beyond the reach of the infinite mercy of the Most Merciful and Most Terrible God.

On the night of the day on which this most

* Cf. "The Imp of the Perverse," vol. v., present edition. —EDITOR.

cruel deed was done, I was aroused from sleep by the cry of fire. The curtains of my bed were in flames. The whole house was blazing. It was with great difficulty that my wife, a servant, and myself, made our escape from the conflagration. The destruction was complete. My entire worldly wealth was swallowed up, and I resigned myself thenceforward to despair.

I am above the weakness of seeking to establish a sequence of cause and effect, between the disaster and the atrocity. But I am detailing a chain of facts—and wish not to leave even a possible link imperfect. On the day succeeding the fire, I visited the ruins. The walls, with one exception, had fallen in. This exception was found in a compartment wall, not very thick, which stood about the middle of the house, and against which had rested the head of my bed. The plastering had here, in great measure, resisted the action of the fire—a fact which I attributed to its having been recently spread. About this wall a dense crowd were collected, and many persons seemed to be examining a particular portion of it with very minute and eager attention. The words "strange!" "singular!" and other similar expressions, excited my curiosity. I approached and saw, as if graven in *bas-relief* upon the white surface, the figure of a gigantic *cat*. The impression was given with an accuracy truly marvellous. There was a rope about the animal's neck.

When I first beheld this apparition—for I could scarcely regard it as less—my wonder and my terror were extreme. But at length reflection came to my aid. The cat, I remembered, had been hung in a garden adjacent to the house. Upon the alarm of fire, this garden had been immediately filled by the crowd—by some one of whom the animal must have been cut from the tree and thrown, through an open window, into my chamber. This had probably been done with the view of arousing me from sleep. The falling of other walls had compressed the victim of my cruelty into the substance of the freshly-spread plaster; the lime of which, with the flames, and the *ammonia* from the carcass, had then accomplished the portraiture as I saw it.

Although I thus readily accounted to my reason, if not altogether to my conscience, for the startling fact just detailed, it did not the less fail to make a deep impression upon my fancy. For months I could not rid myself of the phantasm of the cat; and, during this period, there came back into my spirit a half sentiment that seemed, but was not, remorse. I went so far as to regret the loss of the animal, and to look about me, among the vile haunts which I now habitually frequented, for another pet of the same species, and of somewhat similar appearance, with which to supply its place.

One night as I sat, half stupefied, in a den of more than infamy, my attention was suddenly drawn to some black object, reposing upon the head of one of the immense hogsheads of gin, or of rum, which constituted the chief furniture of the apartment. I had been looking steadily at the top of this hogshead for some minutes, and what now caused me surprise was the fact that I had not sooner perceived the object thereupon. I approached it, and touched it with my hand. It was a black cat—a very large one—fully as large as Pluto, and closely resembling him in every respect but one Pluto had not a white hair upon any portion of his body; but this cat had a large, although indefinite splotch of white, covering nearly the whole region of the breast.

Upon my touching him, he immediately arose, purred loudly, rubbed against my hand, and appeared delighted with my notice. This, then, was the very creature of which I was in search. I at once offered to purchase it of the landlord; but this person made no claim to it—knew nothing of it—had never seen it before.

I continued my caresses, and when I prepared to go home, the animal evinced a disposition to accompany me. I permitted it to do so; occasionally stooping and patting it as I proceeded. When it reached the house it domesticated itself at once, and became immediately a great favorite with my wife.

For my own part, I soon found a dislike to it arising within me. This was just the reverse of what I had anticipated; but—I know not how or why it was—its evident fondness for myself rather disgusted and annoyed me. By slow degrees these feelings of disgust and annoyance rose into the bitterness of hatred. I avoided the creature; a certain sense of shame, and the remembrance of my former deed of cruelty, preventing me from physically abusing it. I did not, for some weeks, strike, or otherwise violently ill use it; but gradually—very gradually—I came to look upon it with unutterable loathing, and to flee silently from its odious presence, as from the breath of a pestilence.

What added, no doubt, to my hatred of the beast, was the discovery, on the morning after I brought it home, that, like Pluto, it also had been deprived of one of its eyes. This circumstance, however, only endeared it to my wife, who, as I have already said, possessed, in a high degree, that humanity of feeling which had once been my distinguishing trait, and the source of many of my simplest and purest pleasures.

With my aversion to this cat, however, its partiality for myself seemed to increase. It followed my footsteps with a pertinacity which it would be difficult to make the reader comprehend. Wherever I sat, it would crouch beneath my chair, or spring upon my knees, covering me with its loathsome caresses. If I arose to walk it would get between my feet and thus nearly throw me down, or, fastening its long and sharp claws in my dress, clamber, in this manner, to my breast. At such times, although I longed to destroy it with a blow, I was yet withheld from so doing, partly by a memory of my former crime, but chiefly—let me confess it at once—by absolute *dread* of the beast.

This dread was not exactly a dread of physical evil—and yet I should be at a loss how otherwise to define it. I am almost ashamed to own—yes, even in this felon's cell, I am almost ashamed to own—that the terror and horror with which the animal inspired me, had been heightened by one of the merest chimeras it would be possible to conceive. My wife had called my attention, more than once, to the character of the mark of white hair, of which I have spoken, and which constituted the sole visible difference between the strange beast and the one I had destroyed. The reader will remember that this mark, although large, had been originally very indefinite; but, by slow degrees—degrees nearly imperceptible, and which for a long time my reason struggled to reject as fanciful—it had, at length, assumed a rigorous distinctness of outline. It was now the representation of an object that I shudder to name—and for this, above all, I loathed, and dreaded, and would have rid myself of the monster *had I dared*—it was now, I say, the image of a hideous—of a ghastly thing—of the GALLOWS! —oh, mournful and terrible engine of Horror and of Crime—of Agony and of Death!

And now was I indeed wretched beyond the wretchedness of mere Humanity. And *a brute beast*—whose fellow I had contemptuously destroyed—*a brute beast* to work out for *me*—for me, a man fashioned in the image of the High God—so much of insufferable woe! Alas! neither by day nor by night knew I the blessing of rest any more! During the former the creature left me no moment alone, and in the latter I started hourly from dreams of unutterable fear to find the hot breath of *the thing* upon my face, and its vast weight—an incarnate nightmare that I had no power to shake off—incumbent eternally upon my *heart!*

Beneath the pressure of torments such as these the feeble remnant of the good within me succumbed. Evil thoughts became my sole intimates—the darkest and most evil of thoughts. The moodiness of my usual temper increased to hatred of all things and of all mankind; while from the sudden, frequent, and ungovernable outbursts of a fury to which I now blindly abandoned myself, my uncomplaining wife, alas! was the most usual and the most patient of sufferers.

One day she accompanied me, upon some household errand, into the cellar of the old building which our poverty compelled us to inhabit. The cat followed me down the steep stairs, and, nearly throwing me headlong, exasperated me to madness. Uplifting an axe, and forgetting in my wrath the childish dread which had hitherto stayed my hand, I aimed a blow at the animal, which, of course, would have proved instantly fatal had it descended as I wished. But this blow was arrested by the hand of my wife. Goaded by the interference into a rage more than demoniacal, I withdrew my arm from her grasp and buried the axe in her brain. She fell dead upon the spot without a groan.

This hideous murder accomplished, I set myself forthwith, and with entire deliberation, to the task of concealing the body. I knew that I could not remove it from the house, either by day or by night, without the risk of being observed by the neighbors. Many projects entered my mind. At one period I thought of cutting the corpse into minute fragments, and destroying them by fire. At another, I resolved to dig a grave for it in the floor of the cellar. Again, I deliberated about casting it in the well in the yard—about packing it in a box, as if merchandise, with the usual arrangements, and so getting a porter to take it from the house. Finally I hit upon what I considered a far better expedient than either of these. I determined to wall it up in the cellar, as the monks of the Middle Ages are recorded to have walled up their victims.

For a purpose such as this the cellar was well adapted. Its walls were loosely constructed, and had lately been plastered throughout with a rough plaster, which the dampness of the atmosphere had prevented from hardening. Moreover, in one of the walls was a projection, caused by a false chimney, or fire-place, that had been filled up and made to resemble the rest of the cellar. I made no doubt that I could readily displace the bricks at this point, insert the corpse, and wall the whole up as before, so that no eye could detect any thing suspicious.

And in this calculation I was not deceived. By means of a crowbar I easily dislodged the bricks, and, having carefully deposited the body against the inner wall, I propped it in that position, while with little trouble I relaid the whole structure as it originally stood. Having procured mortar, sand, and hair, with every possible precaution, I prepared a plaster which could not be distinguished from the old, and with this I very carefully went over the new brick-work. When I had finished, I felt satisfied that all was right. The wall did not present the slightest appearance of having been disturbed. The rubbish on the floor was picked up with the minutest care. I looked around triumphantly, and said to myself: "Here at least, then, my labor has not been in vain."

My next step was to look for the beast which had been the cause of so much wretchedness; for I had, at length, firmly resolved to put it to death. Had I been able to meet with it at the moment, there could have been no doubt of its fate; but it appeared that the crafty animal had been alarmed at the violence of my previous anger, and forebore to present itself in my present mood. It is impossible to describe or to imagine the deep, the blissful sense of relief which the absence of the detested creature occasioned in my bosom. It did not make its appearance during the night; and thus for one night, at least, since its introduction into the house, I soundly and tranquilly slept; aye, *slept* even with the burden of murder upon my soul.

The second and the third day passed, and still my tormentor came not. Once again I breathed as a freeman. The monster, in terror, had fled the premises forever! I should behold it no more! My happiness was supreme! The guilt of my dark deed disturbed me but little. Some few inquiries had been made, but these had been readily answered. Even a search had been instituted—but of course nothing was to be discovered. I looked upon my future felicity as secured.

Upon the fourth day of the assassination, a party of the police came, very unexpectedly, into the house, and proceeded again to make rigorous investigation of the premises. Secure, however, in the inscrutability of my place of concealment, I felt no embarrassment whatever. The officers bade me accompany them in their search. They left no nook or corner unexplored. At length, for the third or fourth time, they descended into the cellar. I quivered not in a muscle. My heart beat calmly as that of one who slumbers in innocence. I walked the cellar from end to end. I folded my arms upon my bosom, and roamed easily to and fro. The police were thoroughly satisfied and prepared to depart. The glee at my heart was too strong to be restrained. I burned to say if but one word, by way of triumph, and to render doubly sure their assurance of my guiltlessness.

"Gentlemen," I said at last, as the party ascended the steps, "I delight to have allayed your suspicions. I wish you all health and a little more courtesy. By the bye, gentlemen, this—this is a very well-constructed house," (in the rabid desire to say something easily, I scarcely knew what I uttered at all),—"I may say an *excellently* well-constructed house. These walls—are you going, gentlemen?—these walls are solidly put together"; and here, through the mere frenzy of bravado, I rapped heavily with a cane which I held in my hand, upon that very portion of the brickwork behind which stood the corpse of the wife of my bosom.

But may God shield and deliver me from the fangs of the Arch-Fiend! No sooner had the reverberation of my blows sunk into silence, than I was answered by a voice from within the tomb! —by a cry, at first muffled and broken, like the sobbing of a child, and then quickly swelling into one long, loud, and continuous scream, utterly anomalous and inhuman—a howl—a wailing shriek, half of horror and half of triumph, such as might have arisen only out of hell, conjointly from the throats of the damned in their agony and of the demons that exult in the damnation.

Of my own thoughts it is folly to speak. Swooning, I staggered to the opposite wall. For one instant the party on the stairs remained motionless, through extremity of terror and awe. In the next a dozen stout arms were toiling at the wall. It fell bodily. The corpse, already greatly decayed and clotted with gore, stood erect before the eyes of the spectators. Upon its head, with red extended mouth and solitary eye of fire, sat the hideous beast whose craft had seduced me into murder, and whose informing voice had consigned me to the hangman. I had walled the monster up within the tomb!

THE FALL OF THE HOUSE OF USHER

[Published in *Burton's Gentleman's Magazine*, September, 1839.]

> Son cœur est un luth suspendu;
> Sitôt qu' on le touche il résonne.
> —*De Beranger.*

DURING the whole of a dull, dark, and soundless day in the autumn of the year, when the clouds hung oppressively low in the heavens, I had been passing alone, on horseback, through a singularly dreary tract of country, and at length found myself, as the shades of the evening drew on, within view of the melancholy House of Usher. I know not how it was—but, with the first glimpse of the building, a sense of insufferable gloom pervaded my spirit. I say insufferable; for the feeling was unrelieved by any of that half-pleasurable, because poetic, sentiment with which the mind usually receives even the sternest natural images of the desolate or terrible. I looked upon the scene before me—upon the mere house, and the simple landscape features of the domain—upon the bleak walls—upon the vacant eye-like windows—upon a few rank sedges—and upon a few white trunks of decayed trees—with an utter depression of soul which I can compare to no earthly sensation more properly than to the after-dream of the reveller upon opium—the bitter lapse into every-day life—the hideous dropping off of the veil. There was an iciness, a sinking, a sickening of the heart—an unredeemed dreariness of thought which no goading of the imagination could torture into aught of the sublime. What was it—I paused to think—what was it that so unnerved me in the contemplation of the House of Usher? It was a mystery all insoluble; nor could I grapple with the shadowy fancies that crowded upon me as I pondered. I was forced to fall back upon the unsatisfactory conclusion, that while, beyond doubt, there *are* combinations of very simple natural objects which have the power of thus affecting us, still the analysis of this power lies among considerations beyond our depth. It was possible, I reflected, that a mere different arrangement of the particulars of the scene, of the details of the picture, would be sufficient to modify, or perhaps to annihilate its capacity for sorrowful impression; and, acting upon this idea, I reined my horse to the precipitous brink of a black and lurid tarn that lay in unruffled lustre by the dwelling, and gazed down—but with a shudder even more thrilling than before—upon the remodelled and inverted images of the gray sedge, and the ghastly tree-stems, and the vacant and eye-like windows.

Nevertheless, in this mansion of gloom I now proposed to myself a sojourn of some weeks. Its proprietor, Roderick Usher, had been one of my boon companions in boyhood; but many years had elapsed since our last meeting. A letter, however, had lately reached me in a distant part of the country—a letter from him—which, in its wildly importunate nature, had admitted of no other than a personal reply. The MS. gave evidence of nervous agitation. The writer spoke of acute bodily illness—of a mental disorder which oppressed him—and of an earnest desire to see me, as his best and indeed his only personal friend, with a view of attempting, by the cheerfulness of my society, some alleviation of his malady. It was the manner in which all this, and much more, was said—it was the apparent *heart* that went with his request—which allowed me no room for hesitation; and I accordingly obeyed forthwith what I still considered a very singular summons.

Although, as boys, we had been even intimate associates, yet I really knew little of my friend. His reserve had been always excessive and habitual. I was aware, however, that his very ancient family had been noted, time out of mind, for a peculiar sensibility of temperament, displaying itself, through long ages, in many works of exalted art, and manifested, of late, in repeated deeds of munificent yet unobtrusive charity, as well as in a passionate devotion to the intricacies, perhaps even more than to the orthodox and easily recognizable beauties, of musical science. I had learned, too, the very remarkable fact, that the stem of the Usher race, all time-honored as it was, had put forth, at no period, any enduring branch; in other words, that the entire family lay in the direct line of descent, and had always, with very trifling and very temporary variations, so lain. It was this deficiency, I considered, while running over in thought the perfect keeping of the character of the premises with the accredited character of the people, and while speculating upon the possible influence which the one, in the long lapse of centuries, might have exercised upon the other—it was this deficiency, perhaps of collateral issue, and the consequent undeviating transmission, from sire to son, of the patrimony with the name, which had, at length so identified the two as to merge the original title of the estate in the quaint and equivocal appellation of the " House of Usher " —an appellation which seemed to include, in the minds of the peasantry who used it, both the family and the family mansion.

I have said that the sole effect of my somewhat childish experiment—that of looking down within the tarn—had been to deepen the first singular impression. There can be no doubt that the consciousness of the rapid increase of my superstition—for why should I not so term it? —served mainly to accelerate the increase itself. Such, I have long known, is the paradoxical law of all sentiments having terror as a basis. And it might have been for this reason only, that, when I again uplifted my eyes to the house itself, from its image in the pool, there grew in my mind a strange fancy—a fancy so ridiculous, indeed, that I but mention it to show the vivid force of the sensations which oppressed me. I had so worked upon my imagination as really to believe that about the whole mansion and domain there hung an atmosphere peculiar to themselves and their immediate vicinity—an atmosphere which had no affinity with the air of heaven, but which had reeked up from the decayed trees, and the gray wall, and the silent tarn—a pestilent and mystic vapor, dull, sluggish, faintly discernible and leaden-hued.

Shaking off from my spirit what *must* have been a dream, I scanned more narrowly the real aspect of the building. Its principal feature seemed to be that of an excessive antiquity. The discoloration of ages had been great. Minute fungi overspread the whole exterior, hanging in a fine tangled web-work from the eaves. Yet all this was apart from any extraordinary dilapidation. No portion of the masonry had fallen; and there appeared to be a wild inconsistency between its still perfect adaptation of parts, and the crumbling condition of the individual stones. In this there was much that reminded me of the specious totality of old wood-work which has rotted for long years in some neglected vault, with no disturbance from the breath of the external air. Beyond this indication of extensive decay, however, the fabric gave little token of instability. Perhaps the eye of a scrutinizing observer might have discovered a barely perceptible fissure, which, extending from the roof of the building in front, made its way down the wall in a zigzag direction, until it became lost in the sullen waters of the tarn.

Noticing these things, I rode over a short causeway to the house. A servant in waiting took my horse, and I entered the Gothic archway of the hall. A valet, of stealthy step, thence conducted me, in silence, through many dark and intricate passages in my progress to the *studio* of his master. Much that I encountered on the way contributed, I know not how, to heighten the vague sentiments of which I have already spoken. While the objects around me—while the carvings of the ceilings, the sombre tapestries of the walls, the ebon blackness of the floors, and the phantasmagoric armorial trophies which rattled as I strode, were but matters to which, or to such as which, I had been accustomed from my infancy—while I hesitated not to acknowledge how familiar was all this—I still wondered to find how unfamiliar were the fancies which ordinary images were stirring up. On one of the staircases, I met the physician of the family. His countenance, I thought, wore a mingled expression of low cunning and perplexity. He accosted me with trepidation and passed on. The valet now threw open a door and ushered me into the presence of his master.

The room in which I found myself was very large and lofty. The windows were long, narrow, and pointed, and at so vast a distance from the black oaken floor as to be altogether inaccessible from within. Feeble gleams of encrimsoned light made their way through the trellised panes, and served to render sufficiently distinct the more prominent objects around; the eye, however, struggled in vain to reach the remoter angles of the chamber, or the recesses of the vaulted and fretted ceiling. Dark draperies hung upon the walls. The general furniture was profuse, comfortless, antique, and tattered. Many books and musical instruments lay scattered about, but failed to give any vitality to the scene. I felt that I breathed an atmosphere of sorrow. An air of stern, deep, and irredeemable gloom hung over and pervaded all.

Upon my entrance, Usher arose from a sofa on which he had been lying at full length, and greeted me with a vivacious warmth which had much in it, I at first thought, of an overdone cordiality—of the constrained effort of the *ennuyé* man of the world. A glance, however, at his countenance convinced me of his perfect sincerity. We sat down; and for some moments, while he spoke not, I gazed upon him with a feeling half of pity, half of awe. Surely, man had never before so terribly altered, in so brief a period, as had Roderick Usher! It was with difficulty that I could bring myself to admit the identity of the wan being before me with the companion of my early boyhood. Yet the character of his face had been at all times remarkable. A cadaverousness of complexion; an eye large, liquid, and luminous beyond comparison; lips somewhat thin and very pallid, but of a surpassingly beautiful curve; a nose of a delicate Hebrew model, but with a breadth of nostril unusual in similar formations; a finely moulded chin, speaking, in its want of prominence, of a want of moral energy; hair of a more than web-like softness and tenuity;—these features, with an inordinate expansion above the regions of the temple, made up altogether a countenance not easily to be forgotten. And now in the mere exaggeration of the prevailing character of these features, and of the expression they were wont to convey, lay so much of change that I doubted to whom I spoke. The now ghastly pallor of the skin, and the now miraculous lustre of the eye, above all things startled and even awed me. The silken hair, too, had been suffered to grow all unheeded, and as, in its wild gossamer texture, it floated rather than fell about the face, I could not, even with effort, connect its Arabesque expression with any idea of simple humanity.

In the manner of my friend I was at once struck with an incoherence—an inconsistency; and I soon found this to arise from a series of feeble and futile struggles to overcome an habitual trepidancy—an excessive nervous agitation. For something of this nature I had indeed been prepared, no less by his letter, than by reminiscences of certain boyish traits, and by conclusions deduced from his peculiar physical conformation and temperament. His action was alternately vivacious and sullen. His voice varied rapidly from a tremulous indecision (when the animal spirits seemed utterly in abeyance) to that species of energetic concision—that abrupt, weighty, un-hurried, and hollow-sounding enunciation—that leaden, self-balanced, and perfectly modulated guttural utterance, which may be observed in the lost drunkard, or the irreclaimable eater of opium, during the periods of his most intense excitement.

It was thus that he spoke of the object of my visit, of his earnest desire to see me, and of the solace he expected me to afford him. He entered, at some length, into what he conceived to be the nature of his malady. It was, he said, a constitutional and a family evil and one for which he despaired to find a remedy—a mere nervous affection, he immediately added, which would undoubtedly soon pass off. It displayed itself in a host of unnatural sensations. Some of these, as he detailed them, interested and bewildered me; although, perhaps, the terms and the general manner of their narration had their weight. He suffered much from a morbid acuteness of the senses; the most insipid food was alone endurable; he could wear only garments of certain texture; the odors of all flowers were oppressive; his eyes were tortured by even a faint light; and there were but peculiar sounds, and these from stringed instruments, which did not inspire him with horror.

To an anomalous species of terror I found him a bounden slave. "I shall perish," said he, "I *must* perish in this deplorable folly. Thus, thus, and not otherwise, shall I be lost. I dread the events of the future, not in themselves, but in their results. I shudder at the thought of any, even the most trivial, incident, which may operate upon this intolerable agitation of soul. I have, indeed, no abhorrence of danger, except in its absolute effect—in terror. In this unnerved, in this pitiable, condition I feel that the period will sooner or later arrive when I must abandon life and reason together, in some struggle with the grim phantasm, FEAR."

I learned, moreover, at intervals, and through broken and equivocal hints, another singular feature of his mental condition. He was enchained by certain superstitious impressions in regard to the dwelling which he tenanted, and whence, for many years, he had never ventured forth—in regard to an influence whose supposititious force was conveyed in terms too shadowy here to be restated—an influence which some peculiarities in the mere form and substance of his family mansion had, by dint of long sufferance, he said, obtained over his spirit—an effect which the *physique* of the gray walls and turrets, and of the dim tarn into which they all looked down, had, at length, brought about upon the *morale* of his existence.

He admitted, however, although with hesitation, that much of the peculiar gloom which thus afflicted him could be traced to a more natural and far more palpable origin—to the severe and long-continued illness—indeed to the evidently approaching dissolution—of a tenderly beloved sister, his sole companion for long years, his last and only relative on earth. "Her decease," he said, with a bitterness which I can never forget, "would leave him (him, the hopeless and the frail) the last of the ancient race of the Ushers." While he spoke, the lady Madeline (for so was she called) passed through a remote portion of the apartment, and, without having noticed my presence, disappeared. I regarded her with an utter astonishment not unmingled with dread; and yet I found it impossible to account for such feelings. A sensation of stupor oppressed me as my eyes followed her retreating steps. When a door, at length, closed upon her, my glance sought instinctively and eagerly the countenance of the brother; but he had buried his face in his hands, and I could only perceive that a far more than ordinary wanness had overspread the emaciated fingers through which trickled many passionate tears.

The disease of the lady Madeline had long baffled the skill of her physicians. A settled apathy, a gradual wasting away of the person, and frequent although transient affections of a partially cataleptical character were the unusual diagnosis. Hitherto she had steadily borne up against the pressure of her malady, and had not betaken herself finally to bed; but on the closing in of the evening of my arrival at the house, she succumbed (as her brother told me at night with inexpressible agitation) to the prostrating power of the destroyer; and I learned that the glimpse I had obtained in her person would thus probably be the last I should obtain—that the lady, at least while living, would be seen by me no more.

For several days ensuing, her name was unmentioned by either Usher or myself; and during this period I was busied in earnest endeavors to alleviate the melancholy of my friend. We painted and read together, or I listened, as if in a dream, to the wild improvisations of his speaking guitar. And thus, as a closer and still closer intimacy admitted me more unreservedly into the recesses of his spirit, the more bitterly did I perceive the futility of all attempts at cheering a mind from which darkness, as if an inherent positive quality, poured forth upon all objects of the moral and physical universe in one unceasing radiation of gloom.

I shall ever bear about me a memory of the many solemn hours I thus spent alone with the master of the House of Usher. Yet I should fail in any attempt to convey an idea of the exact character of the studies, or of the occupations, in which he involved me, or led me the way. An excited and highly distempered ideality threw a sulphurous lustre over all. His long improvised dirges will ring forever in my ears. Among other things, I hold painfully in mind a certain singular perversion and amplification of the wild air of the last waltz of Von Weber. From the paintings over which his elaborate fancy brooded, and which grew, touch by touch, into vaguenesses at which I shuddered the more thrillingly, because I shuddered knowing not why—from these paintings (vivid as their images now are before me) I would in vain endeavor to educe more than a small portion which should lie within the compass of merely written words. By the utter simplicity, by the nakedness of his designs, he arrested and overawed attention. If ever mortal painted an idea, that mortal was Roderick Usher. For me at least, in the circumstances then surrounding me, there arose out of the pure abstractions which the hypochondriac contrived to throw upon his canvas, an intensity of intolerable awe, no shadow of which felt I ever yet in the contemplation of the certainly glowing yet too concrete reveries of Fuseli.

One of the phantasmagoric conceptions of my friend, partaking not so rigidly of the spirit of abstraction, may be shadowed forth, although feebly, in words. A small picture presented the interior of an immensely long and rectangular vault or tunnel, with low walls, smooth, white and without interruption or device. Certain accessory points of the design served well to convey the idea that this excavation lay at an exceeding depth below the surface of the earth. No outlet was observed in any portion of its vast extent, and no torch or other artificial source of light was discernible; yet a flood of intense rays rolled throughout, and bathed the whole in a ghastly and inappropriate splendor.

I have just spoken of that morbid condition of the auditory nerve which rendered all music intolerable to the sufferer, with the exception of certain effects of stringed instruments. It was, perhaps, the narrow limits to which he thus confined himself upon the guitar which gave birth, in great measure, to the fantastic character of his performances. But the fervid *facility* of his *impromptus* could not be so accounted for. They must have been, and were, in the notes, as well as in the words of his wild fantasias (for he not unfrequently accompanied himself with rhymed verbal improvisations), the result of that intense mental collectedness and concentration to which I have previously alluded as observable only in particular moments of the highest artificial excitement. The words of one of these rhapsodies I have easily remembered. I was, perhaps, the more forcibly impressed with it as he gave it, because, in the under or mystic current of its meaning, I fancied that I perceived, and for the first time, a full consciousness on the part of Usher of the tottering of his lofty reason upon her throne. The verses, which were entitled "The Haunted Palace," ran very nearly, if not accurately, thus:—

I.

In the greenest of our valleys,
  By good angels tenanted,
Once a fair and stately palace—
  Radiant palace—reared its head.
In the monarch Thought's dominion—
  It stood there!
Never seraph spread a pinion
  Over fabric half so fair.

II.

Banners yellow, glorious, golden,
  On its roof did float and flow
(This—all this—was in the olden
  Time long ago);
And every gentle air that dallied,
  In that sweet day,
Along the ramparts plumed and pallid,
  A winged odor went away.

III.

Wanderers in that happy valley
  Through two luminous windows saw
Spirits moving musically
  To a lute's well tunéd law;
Round about a throne, where sitting
  (Porphyrogene!)
In state his glory well befitting,
  The ruler of the realm was seen.

IV.

And all with pearl and ruby glowing
  Was the fair palace door,
Through which came flowing, flowing, flowing
  And sparkling evermore,
A troop of Echoes whose sweet duty
  Was but to sing,
In voices of surpassing beauty,
  The wit and wisdom of their king.

V.

But evil things, in robes of sorrow,
  Assailed the monarch's high estate;
(Ah, let us mourn, for never morrow
  Shall dawn upon him, desolate!)
And, round about his home, the glory
  That blushed and bloomed
Is but a dim-remembered story
  Of the old time entombed.

VI.

And travellers now within that valley,
  Through the red-litten windows see
Vast forms that move fantastically
  To a discordant melody;
While, like a rapid ghastly river,
  Through the pale door,
A hideous throng rush out forever,
  And laugh—but smile no more.

I well remember that suggestions arising from this ballad led us into a train of thought wherein there became manifest an opinion of Usher's, which I mention not so much on account of its novelty (for other men* have thought thus), as

* Watson, Dr. Percival, Spallanzani, and especially the Bishop of Landaff.—See "Chemical Essays," vol. v.

on account of the pertinacity with which he maintained it. This opinion, in its general form, was that of the sentience of all vegetable things. But, in his disordered fancy, the idea had assumed a more daring character, and trespassed, under certain conditions, upon the kingdom of inorganization. I lack words to express the full extent, or the earnest *abandon* of his persuasion. The belief, however, was connected (as I have previously hinted) with the gray stones of the home of his forefathers. The conditions of the sentence had been here, he imagined, fulfilled in the method of collocation of these stones—in the order of their arrangement, as well as in that of the many *fungi* which overspread them, and of the decayed trees which stood around—above all, in the long undisturbed endurance of this arrangement, and in its reduplication in the still waters of the tarn. Its evidence—the evidence of the sentience—was to be seen, he said (and I here started as he spoke), in the gradual yet certain condensation of an atmosphere of their own about the waters and the walls. The result was discoverable, he added, in that silent yet importunate and terrible influence which for centuries had moulded the destinies of his family, and which made *him* what I now saw him—what he was. Such opinions need no comment, and I will make none.

Our books—the books which, for years, had formed no small portion of the mental existence of the invalid—were, as might be supposed, in strict keeping with this character of phantasm.

We pored together over such works as the "Ververt et Chartreuse" of Gresset; the "Belphegor" of Machiavelli; the "Heaven and Hell" of Swedenborg; the "Subterranean Voyage of Nicholas Klimm" by Holberg; the "Chiromancy" of Robert Flud, of Jean D'Indaginé and of De la Chambre; the "Journey into the Blue Distance of Tieck"; and the "City of the Sun" of Campanella. One favorite volume was a small octavo edition of the "Directorium Inquisitorum," by the Dominican Eymeric de Gironne; and there were passages in Pomponius Mela, about the old African Satyrs and Ægipans, over which Usher would sit dreaming for hours. His chief delight, however, was found in the perusal of an exceedingly rare and curious book in quarto Gothic—the manual of a forgotten church—the *Vigiliæ Mortuorum secundum Chorum Ecclesiæ Maguntinæ.*

I could not help thinking of the wild ritual of this work, and of its probable influence upon the hypochondriac, when, one evening, having informed me abruptly that the lady Madeline was no more, he stated his intention of preserving her corpse for a fortnight (previously to its final interment), in one of the numerous vaults within the main walls of the building. The worldly reason, however, assigned for this singular proceeding, was one which I did not feel at liberty to dispute. The brother had been led to his resolution (so he told me) by consideration of the unusual character of the malady of the deceased, of certain obtrusive and eager inquiries on the part of her medical men, and of the remote and exposed situation of the burial-ground of the family. I will not deny that when I called to mind the sinister countenance of the person whom I met upon the staircase, on the day of my arrival at the house, I had no desire to oppose what I regarded as at best but a harmless, and by no means an unnatural, precaution.

At the request of Usher, I personally aided him in the arangements for the temporary entombment. The body having been encoffined, we two alone bore it to its rest. The vault in which we placed it (and which had been so long unopened that our torches, half smothered in its oppressive atmosphere, gave us little opportunity for investigation) was small, damp, and entirely without means of admission for light; lying, at great depth, immediately beneath that portion of the building in which was my own sleeping apartment. It had been used, apparently, in remote feudal times, for the worst purposes of a donjon-keep, and, in later days, as a place of deposit for powder, or some other highly combustible substance, as a portion of its floor, and the whole interior of a long archway through which we reached it, were carefully sheathed with copper. The door, of massive iron, had been, also, similarly protected. Its immense weight caused an unusually sharp, grating sound, as it moved upon its hinges.

Having deposited our mournful burden upon tressels within this region of horror, we partially turned aside the yet unscrewed lid of the coffin, and looked upon the face of the tenant. A striking similitude between the brother and sister now first arrested my attention; and Usher, divining, perhaps, my thoughts, murmured out some few words from which I learned that the deceased and himself had been twins, and that sympathies of a scarcely intelligible nature had always existed between them. Our glances, however, rested not long upon the dead—for we could not regard her unawed. The disease which had thus entombed the lady in the maturity of youth, had left, as usual in all maladies of a strictly cataleptical character, the mockery of a faint blush upon the bosom and the face, and that suspiciously lingering smile upon the lip which is so terrible in death. We replaced and screwed down the lid, and, having secured the door of iron, made our way, with toil, into the scarcely less gloomy apartments of the upper portion of the house.

And now, some days of bitter grief having elapsed, an observable change came over the features of the mental disorder of my friend. His ordinary manner had vanished. His ordinary occupations were neglected or forgotten. He roamed from chamber to chamber with hurried, unequal, and objectless step. The pallor of his countenance had assumed, if possible, a more ghastly hue—but the luminousness of his eye had utterly gone out. The once occasional huskiness of his tone was heard no more; and a tremulous quaver, as if of extreme terror, habitually characterized his utterance. There were times, indeed, when I thought his unceasingly agitated mind was laboring with some oppressive secret, to divulge which he struggled for the necessary courage. At times, again, I was obliged to resolve all into the mere inexplicable vagaries of madness, for I beheld him gazing upon vacancy for long hours, in an attitude of the profoundest attention, as if listening to some imaginary sound. It was no wonder that his condition terrified—that it infected me. I felt creeping upon me, by slow yet certain degrees, the wild influences of his own fantastic yet impressive superstitions.

It was, especially, upon retiring to bed late in the night of the seventh or eighth day after the placing of the lady Madeline within the donjon, that I experienced the full power of such feelings. Sleep came not near my couch—while the hours waned and waned away. I struggled to reason off the nervousness which had dominion over me. I endeavored to believe that much, if not all of what I felt, was due to the bewildering influence of the gloomy furniture of the room—of the dark and tattered draperies, which, tortured into motion by the breath of a rising tempest, swayed fitfully to and fro upon the walls, and rustled uneasily about the decorations of the bed. But my efforts were fruitless. An irrepressible tremor gradually pervaded my frame; and, at length, there sat upon my very heart an incubus of utterly causeless alarm. Shaking this off with a gasp and a struggle, I uplifted myself upon the pillows, and, peering earnestly within the intense darkness of the chamber, hearkened —I know not why, except that an instinctive spirit prompted me—to certain low and indefinite sounds which came, through the pauses of the storm, at long intervals, I knew not whence. Overpowered by an intense sentiment of horror, unaccountable yet unendurable, I threw on my clothes with haste (for I felt that I should sleep no more during the night), and endeavored to arouse myself from the pitiable condition into which I had fallen, by pacing rapidly to and fro through the apartment.

I had taken but few turns in this manner, when a light step on an adjoining staircase arrested my attention. I presently recognized it as that of Usher. In an instant afterward he rapped, with a gentle touch, at my door, and entered, bearing a lamp. His countenance was, as usual, cadaverously wan—but, moreover, there was a species of mad hilarity in his eyes—an evidently restrained *hysteria* in his whole demeanor. His air appalled me—but any thing was preferable to the solitude which I had so long endured, and I even welcomed his presence as a relief.

"And you have not seen it?" he said abruptly, after having stared about him for some moments in silence—"you have not then seen it?—but, stay! you shall." Thus speaking, and having carefully shaded his lamp, he hurried to one of the casements, and threw it freely open to the storm.

The impetuous fury of the entering gust nearly lifted us from our feet. It was, indeed, a tempestuous yet sternly beautiful night, and one wildly singular in its terror and its beauty. A whirlwind had apparently collected its force in our vicinity; for there were frequent and violent alterations in the direction of the wind; and the exceeding density of the clouds (which hung so low as to press upon the turrets of the house) did not prevent our perceiving the lifelike velocity with which they flew careering from all points against each other, without passing away into the distance. I say that even their exceeding density did not prevent our perceiving this —yet we had no glimpse of the moon or stars, nor was there any flashing forth of the lightning. But the under surfaces of the huge masses of agitated vapor, as well as all terrestrial objects immediately around us, were glowing in the unnatural light of a faintly luminous and distinctly visible gaseous exhalation which hung about and enshrouded the mansion.

"You must not—you shall not behold this!" said I, shuddering, to Usher, as I led him, with a gentle violence, from the window to a seat. "These appearances, which bewilder you, are merely electrical phenomena not uncommon —or it may be that they have their ghastly origin in the rank miasma of the tarn. Let us close this casement;—the air is chilling and dangerous to your frame. Here is one of your favorite romances. I will read, and you shall listen:— and so we will pass away this terrible night together."

The antique volume which I had taken up was the "Mad Trist" of Sir Launcelot Canning; but I had called it a favorite of Usher's more in sad jest than in earnest; for, in truth, there is little in its uncouth and unimaginative prolixity which could have had interest for the lofty and spiritual ideality of my friend. It was, however, the only book immediately at hand; and I indulged a vague hope that the excitement which now agitated the hypochondriac, might find relief (for the history of mental disorder is full of similar anomalies) even in the extremeness of the folly which I should read. Could I have judged, indeed, by the wild overstrained air of vivacity with which he hearkened, or apparently hearkened, to the words of the tale, I might well have congratulated myself upon the success of my design.

I had arrived at that well-known portion of the story where Ethelred, the hero of the Trist, having sought in vain for peaceable admission into the dwelling of the hermit, proceeds to make good an entrance by force. Here, it will be remembered, the words of the narrative run thus:

And Ethelred, who was by nature of a doughty heart, and who was now mighty withal, on account of the powerfulness of the wine which he had drunken, waited no longer to hold parley with the hermit, who, in sooth, was of an obstinate and maliceful turn, but, feeling the rain upon his shoulders, and fearing the rising of the tempest, uplifted his mace outright, and, with blows, made quickly room in the plankings of the door for his gauntleted hand; and now pulling therewith sturdily, he so cracked, and ripped, and tore all asunder, that the noise of the dry and hollow-sounding wood alarumed and reverberated throughout the forest.

At the termination of this sentence I started and, for a moment, paused; for it appeared to me (although I at once concluded that my excited fancy had deceived me)—it appeared to me that, from some very remote portion of the mansion, there came, indistinctly to my ears, what might have been, in its exact similarity of character, the echo (but a stifled and dull one certainly) of the very cracking and ripping sound which Sir Launcelot had so particularly described. It was, beyond doubt, the coincidence alone which had arrested my attention; for, amid the rattling of the sashes of the casements, and the ordinary commingled noises of the still increasing storm, the sound, in itself, had nothing, surely, which should have interested or disturbed me. I continued the story:

But the good champion Ethelred, now entering within the door, was sore enraged and amazed to perceive no signal of the maliceful hermit; but, in the stead thereof, a dragon of a scaly and prodigious demeanor, and of a fiery tongue, which sate in guard before a palace of gold, with a floor of silver; and upon the wall there hung a shield of shining brass with this legend enwritten—

Who entereth herein, a conqueror hath bin;
Who slayeth the dragon, the shield he shall win.

And Ethelred uplifted his mace, and struck upon the head of the dragon, which fell before him, and gave up his pesty breath, with a shriek so horrid and harsh, and withal so piercing, that Ethelred had fain to close his ears with his hands against the dreadful noise of it, the like whereof was never before heard.

Here again I paused abruptly, and now with a feeling of wild amazement—for there could be no doubt whatever that, in this instance, I did actually hear (although from what direction it proceeded I found it impossible to say) a low and apparently distant, but harsh, protracted, and most unusual screaming or grating sound—the exact counterpart of what my fancy had already conjured up for the dragon's unnatural shriek as described by the romancer.

Oppressed, as I certainly was, upon the occurrence of this second and most extraordinary coincidence, by a thousand conflicting sensations, in which wonder and extreme terror were predominant, I still retained sufficient presence of mind to avoid exciting, by an observation, the sensitive nervousness of my companion. I was by no means certain that he had noticed the sounds in question; although, assuredly, a strange alteration had, during the last few minutes, taken place in his demeanor. From a position fronting my own, he had gradually brought round his chair, so as to sit with his face to the door of the chamber; and thus I could but partially perceive his features, although I saw that his lips trembled as if he were murmuring inaudibly. His head had dropped upon his breast—yet I knew that he was not asleep, from the wide and rigid opening of the eye as I caught a glance of it in profile. The motion of his body, too, was at variance with this idea—for he rocked from side to side with a gentle yet constant and uniform sway. Having rapidly taken notice of all this, I resumed the narrative of Sir Launcelot, which thus proceeded:

And now, the champion, having escaped from the terrible fury of the dragon, bethinking himself of the brazen shield, and of the breaking up of the enchantment which was upon it, removed the carcass from out of the way before him, and approached valorously over the silver pavement of the castle to where the shield was upon the wall; which in sooth tarried not for his full coming, but fell down at his feet upon the silver floor, with a mighty great and terrible ringing sound.

No sooner had these syllables passed my lips, than—as if a shield of brass had indeed, at the moment, fallen heavily upon a floor of silver—I became aware of a distinct, hollow, metallic, and clangorous, yet apparently, muffled, reverberation. Completely unnerved, I leaped to my feet; but the measured rocking movement of Usher was undisturbed. I rushed to the chair in which he sat. His eyes were bent fixedly before him, and throughout his whole countenance there reigned a stony rigidity. But, as I placed my hand upon his shoulder, there came a strong shudder over his whole person; a sickly smile quivered about his lips; and I saw that he spoke in a low, hurried, and gibbering murmur, as if unconscious of my presence. Bending closely over him I at length drank in the hideous import of his words.

"Not hear it?—yes, I hear it, and *have* heard

it. Long—long—long—many minutes, many hours, many days, have I heard it—yet I dared not—oh, pity me, miserable wretch that I am! —I dared not—I *dared* not speak! *We have put her living in the tomb!* Said I not that my senses were acute? I *now* tell you that I heard her first feeble movements in the hollow coffin. I heard them—many, many days ago—yet I dared not—*I dared not speak!* And now—to-night—Ethelred—ha! ha!—the breaking of the hermit's door, and the death-cry of the dragon, and the clangor of the shield—say, rather, the rending of her coffin, and the grating of the iron hinges of her prison, and her struggles within the coppered archway of the vault! Oh! whither shall I fly? Will she not be here anon? Is she not hurrying to upbraid me for my haste? Have I not heard her footstep on the stair? Do I not distinguish that heavy and horrible beating of her heart? Madman!"—here he sprang furiously to his feet, and shrieked out his syllables, as if in the effort he were giving up his soul—"*Madman! I tell you that she now stands without the door!*"

As if in the superhuman energy of his utterance there had been found the potency of a spell, the huge antique panels to which the speaker pointed threw slowly back, upon the instant, their ponderous and ebony jaws. It was the work of the rushing gust—but then without those doors there *did* stand the lofty and enshrouded figure of the lady Madeline of Usher. There was blood upon her white robes, and the evidence of some bitter struggle upon every portion of her emaciated frame. For a moment she remained trembling and reeling to and fro upon the threshold—then, with a low moaning cry, fell heavily inward upon the person of her brother, and in her violent and now final death-agonies, bore him to the floor a corpse, and a victim to the terrors he had anticipated.

From that chamber, and from that mansion, I fled aghast. The storm was still abroad in all its wrath as I found myself crossing the old causeway. Suddenly there shot along the path a wild light, and I turned to see whence a gleam so unusual could have issued, for the vast house and its shadows were alone behind me. The radiance was that of the full, setting, and blood-red moon, which now shone vividly through that once barely discernible fissure, of which I have before spoken as extending from the roof of the building, in a zigzag direction, to the base. While I gazed, this fissure rapidly widened—there came a fierce breath of the whirlwind—the entire orb of the satellite burst at once upon my sight—my brain reeled as I saw the mighty walls rushing asunder—there was a long tumultuous shouting sound like the voice of a thousand waters—and the deep and dank tarn at my feet closed sullenly and silently over the fragments of the "*House of Usher.*"

BERENICE

[Published in the *Southern Literary Messenger,* March, 1835.]

Dicebant mihi sodales, si sepulchrum amicæ visitarem, curas meas aliquantulum fore levatas.—*Ebn Zaiat.*

MISERY is manifold. The wretchedness of earth is multiform. Overreaching the wide horizon as the rainbow, its hues are as various as the hues of that arch—as distinct too, yet as intimately blended. Overreaching the wide horizon as the rainbow! How is it that from beauty I have derived a type of unloveliness?—from the covenant of peace, a smile of sorrow? But, as in ethics, evil is a consequence of good, so, in fact, out of joy is sorrow born. Either the memory of past bliss is the anguish of to-day, or the agonies which *are,* have their origin in the ecstasies which *might have been.*

My baptismal name is Egæus; that of my family I will not mention. Yet there are no towers in the land more time-honored than my gloomy, gray, hereditary halls. Our line has been called a race of visionaries; and in many striking particulars—in the character of the family mansion—in the frescoes of the chief saloon—in the tapestries of the dormitories—in the chiselling of some buttresses in the armory—but more especially in the gallery of antique paintings—in the fashion of the library chamber—and, lastly, in the very peculiar nature of the library's contents—there is more than sufficient evidence to warrant the belief.

The recollections of my earliest years are connected with that chamber, and with its volumes—of which latter I will say no more. Here died my mother. Herein was I born. But it is mere idleness to say that I had not lived before—that the soul has no previous existence. You deny it?—let us not argue the matter. Convinced myself, I seek not to convince. There is, however, a remembrance of aërial forms—of spiritual and meaning eyes—of sounds, musical yet sad; a remembrance which will not be excluded; a memory like a shadow—vague, variable, indefinite, unsteady; and like a shadow, too, in the impossibility of my getting rid of it while the sunlight of my reason shall exist.

In that chamber was I born. Thus awaking from the long night of what seemed, but was not, nonentity, at once into the very regions of fairy land—into a palace of imagination—into the wild dominions of monastic thought and erudition—it is not singular that I gazed around me with a startled and ardent eye—that I loitered away my boyhood in books, and dissipated my youth in revery; but it *is* singular, that as years rolled away, and the noon of manhood found me still in the mansion of my fathers—it *is* wonderful what a stagnation there fell upon the springs of my life—wonderful how total an inversion took place in the character of my commonest thought. The realities of the world affected me as visions, and as visions only, while the wild ideas of the land of dreams became, in turn, not the material of my every-day existence, but in very deed that existence utterly and solely in itself.

* * * * * * *

Berenice and I were cousins, and we grew up together in my paternal halls. Yet differently we grew—I, ill of health, and buried in gloom—she, agile, graceful, and overflowing with energy; hers the ramble on the hill-side—mine, the studies of the cloister; I, living within my own heart, and addicted, body and soul, to the most intense and painful meditation—she, roaming carelessly through life, with no thought of the shadows in her path, or the silent flight of the raven-winged hours. Berenice!—I call upon her name—Berenice!—and from the gray ruins of memory a thousand tumultuous recollections are startled at the sound! Ah, vividly is her image before me now, as in the early days of her light-heartedness and joy! Oh, gorgeous yet fantastic beauty! Oh, sylph amid the shrubberies of Arnheim! Oh, naiad among its fountains! And then—then all is mystery and terror, and a tale which should not be told. Disease—a fatal disease, fell like the simoon upon her frame; and even, while I gazed upon her, the spirit of change swept over her, pervading her mind, her habits, and her character, and, in a manner the most subtle and terrible, disturbing even the identity of her person! Alas! the destroyer came and went!—and the victim—where is she? I knew her not—or knew her no longer as Berenice!

Among the numerous train of maladies superinduced by that fatal and primary one which effected a revolution of so horrible a kind in the moral and physical being of my cousin, may be mentioned as the most distressing and obstinate in its nature, a species of epilepsy not unfrequently terminating in *trance* itself—trance very nearly resembling positive dissolution, and from which her manner of recovery was, in most instances, startlingly abrupt. In the meantime, my own disease—for I have been told that I should call it by no other appellation—my own disease, then, grew rapidly upon me, and assumed finally a monomaniac character of a novel and extraordinary form—hourly and momently gaining vigor—and at length obtaining over me the most incomprehensible ascendancy. This monomania, if I must so term it, consisted in a morbid irritability of those properties of the mind in metaphysical science termed the *attentive*. It is more than probable that I am not understood; but I fear, indeed, that it is in no manner possible to convey to the mind of the merely general reader, an adequate idea of that nervous *intensity of interest* with which, in my case, the powers of meditation (not to speak technically) busied and buried themselves, in the contemplation of even the most ordinary objects of the universe.

To muse for long unwearied hours, with my attention riveted to some frivolous device on the margin or in the typography of a book; to become absorbed, for the better part of a summer's day, in a quaint shadow falling aslant upon the tapestry or upon the floor; to lose myself, for an entire night, in watching the steady flame of a lamp, or the embers of a fire, to dream away whole days over the perfume of a flower; to repeat, monotonously, some common word, until the sound, by dint of frequent repetition, ceased to convey any idea whatever to the mind; to lose all sense of motion or physical existence, by means of absolute bodily quiescence long and obstinately persevered in: such were a few of the most common and least pernicious vagaries induced by a condition of the mental faculties, not, indeed, although unparalleled, but certainly bidding defiance to any thing like analysis or explanation.

Yet let me not be misapprehended. The undue, earnest, and morbid attention thus excited by objects in their own nature frivolous, must not be confounded in character with that ruminating propensity common to all mankind, and more especially indulged in by persons of ardent imagination. It was not even, as might be at first supposed, an extreme condition, or exaggeration of such propensity, but primarily and essentially distinct and different. In the one instance, the dreamer, or enthusiast, being interested by an object usually *not* frivolous, imperceptibly loses sight of this object in a wilderness of deductions and suggestions issuing therefrom, until, at the conclusion of a day-dream *often replete with luxury,* he finds the *incitamentum,* or first cause of his musings, entirely vanished and forgotten. In my case, the primary object was *invariably frivolous,* although assuming, through the medium of my distempered vision, a refracted and unreal importance. Few deductions, if any, were made; and those few pertinaciously returning in upon the original object as a centre. The meditations were *never* pleasurable; and, at the termination of the revery, the first cause, so far from being out of sight, had attained that supernaturally exaggerated interest which was the prevailing feature of the disease. In a word, the powers of mind more particularly exercised were, with me, as I have said before, the *attentive,* and are, with the day-dreamer, the *speculative.*

My books, at this epoch, if they did not actually serve to irritate the disorder, partook, it will be perceived, largely, in their imaginative and inconsequential nature, of the characteristic qualities of the disorder itself. I well remember, among others, the treatise of the noble Italian, Cœlius Secundus Curio, "*De Amplitudine Beati Regni Dei*"; St. Austin's great work, "The City of God"; and Tertullian's "*De Carne Christi,*" in which the paradoxical sentence, "*Mortuus est Dei filius; credibile est quia ineptum est; et sepultus resurrexit; certum est quia impossible est,"* occupied my undivided time, for many weeks of laborious and fruitless investigation.

Thus it will appear that, shaken from its balance only by trivial things, my reason bore resemblance to that ocean-crag spoken of by Ptolemy Hephestion, which steadily resisting the attacks of human violence, and the fiercer fury of the waters and the winds, trembled only to the touch of the flower called Asphodel. And although, to a careless thinker, it might appear a matter beyond doubt, that the alteration produced by her unhappy malady, in the *moral* condition of Berenice, would afford me many objects for the exercise of that intense and abnormal meditation whose nature I have been at some trouble in explaining, yet such was not in any degree the case. In the lucid intervals of my infirmity, her calamity, indeed, gave me pain, and, taking deeply to heart that total wreck of her fair and gentle life, I did not fail to ponder, frequently and bitterly, upon the wonder-working means by which so strange a revolution had been so suddenly brought to pass. But these reflections partook not of the idiosyncrasy of my disease, and were such as would have occurred, under similar circumstances, to the ordinary mass of mankind. True to its own character, my disorder revelled in the less important but more startling changes wrought in the *physical* frame of Berenice—in the singular and most appalling distortion of her personal identity.

During the brightest days of her unparalleled

beauty, most surely I had never loved her. In the strange anomaly of my existence, feelings with me, *had never been* of the heart, and my passions *always were* of the mind. Through the gray of the early morning—among the trellised shadows of the forest at noonday—and in the silence of my library at night—she had flitted by my eyes, and I had seen her—not as the living and breathing Berenice, but as the Berenice of a dream; not as a being of the earth, earthly, but as the abstraction of such a being; not as a thing to admire, but to analyze; not as an object of love, but as the theme of the most abstruse although desultory speculation. And *now*—now I shuddered in her presence, and grew pale at her approach; yet, bitterly lamenting her fallen and desolate condition, I called to mind that she had loved me long, and, in an evil moment, I spoke to her of marriage.

And at length the period of our nuptials was approaching, when, upon an afternoon in the winter of the year—one of those unseasonably warm, calm, and misty days which are the nurse of the beautiful Halcyon,*—I sat (and sat, as I thought, alone) in the inner apartment of the library. But uplifting my eyes, I saw that Berenice stood before me.

Was it my own excited imagination—or the misty influence of the atmosphere—or the uncertain twilight of the chamber—or the gray

* For as Jove, during the winter season, gives twice seven days of warmth, men have called this clement and temperate time the nurse of the beautiful Halcyon.—*Simonides.*

draperies which fell around her figure—that caused in it so vacillating and indistinct an outline? I could not tell. She spoke no word; and I—not for worlds could I have uttered a syllable. An icy chill ran through my frame; a sense of insufferable anxiety oppressed me; a consuming curiosity pervaded my soul; and, sinking back upon the chair, I remained for some time breathless and motionless, with my eyes riveted upon her person. Alas! its emaciation was excessive, and not one vestige of the former being lurked in any single line of the contour. My burning glances at length fell upon the face.

The forehead was high, and very pale, and singularly placid; and the once jetty hair fell partially over it, and overshadowed the hollow temples with innumerable ringlets, now of a vivid yellow, and jarring discordantly, in their fantastic character, with the reigning melancholy of the countenance. The eyes were lifeless, and lustreless, and seemingly pupilless, and I shrank involuntarily from their glassy stare to the contemplation of the thin and shrunken lips. They parted; and in a smile of peculiar meaning, *the teeth* of the changed Berenice disclosed themselves slowly to my view. Would to God that I had never beheld them, or that, having done so, I had died!

* * * * * * *

The shutting of a door disturbed me, and looking up, I found that my cousin had departed from the chamber. But from the disordered chamber of my brain, had not, alas! departed, and would not be driven away, the white and ghastly *spectrum* of the teeth. Not a speck on their surface—not a shade on their enamel—not an indenture in their edges—but what the brief period of her smile had sufficed to brand in upon my memory. I saw them *now* even more unequivocally than I beheld them *then*. The teeth! —the teeth!—they were here, and there, and everywhere, and visibly and palpably before me; long, narrow, and excessively white, with the pale lips writhing about them, as in the very moment of their first terrible development. Then came the full fury of my *monomania*, and I struggled in vain against its strange and irresistible influence. In the multiplied objects of the external world I had no thoughts but for the teeth. For these I longed with a frenzied desire. All other matters and all different interests became absorbed in their single contemplation. They—they alone were present to the mental eye, and they, in their sole individuality, became the essence of my mental life. I held them in every light. I turned them in every attitude. I surveyed their characteristics. I dwelt upon their peculiarities. I pondered upon their conformation. I mused upon the alteration in their nature. I shuddered as I assigned to them, in imagination, a sensitive and sentient power, and even when unassisted by the lips, a capability of moral expression. Of Mademoiselle Sallé it has been well said: "*Que tous ses pas étaient des sentiments,*" and of Berenice I more seriously believed *que tous ses dents étaient des idées. Des idées!*—ah, here was the idiotic thought that destroyed me! *Des idées!*—ah *therefore* it was that I coveted them so madly! I felt that their possession could alone ever restore me to peace, in giving me back to reason.

And the evening closed in upon me thus—and then the darkness came, and tarried, and went—and the day again dawned—and the mists of a second night were now gathering around—and still I sat motionless in that solitary room—and still I sat buried in meditation—and still the *phantasma* of the teeth maintained its terrible ascendancy, as, with the most vivid and hideous distinctness, it floated about amid the changing lights and shadows of the chamber. At length there broke in upon my dreams a cry as of horror and dismay; and thereunto, after a pause, succeeded the sound of troubled voices, intermingled with many low moanings of sorrow or of pain. I arose from my seat, and throwing open one of the doors of the library, saw standing out in the antechamber a servant maiden, all in tears, who told me that Berenice was—no more! She had been seized with epilepsy in the early morning, and now, at the closing in of the night, the grave was ready for its tenant, and all the preparations for the burial were completed.

* * * * * * *

I found myself sitting in the library, and again sitting there alone. It seemed to me that I had newly awakened from a confused and exciting dream. I knew that it was now midnight, and I was well aware, that since the setting of the sun, Berenice had been interred. But of that dreary period which intervened I had no positive, at least no definite, comprehension. Yet its memory was replete with horror—horror more horrible from being vague, and terror more terrible from ambiguity. It was a fearful page in the record of my existence, written all over with dim, and hideous, and unintelligible recollections. I strived to decipher them, but in vain; while ever and anon, like the spirit of a departed sound, the shrill and piercing shriek of a female voice seemed to be ringing in my ears. I had done a deed—what was it? I asked myself the question aloud, and the whispering echoes of the chamber answered me—"*What was it?*"

On the table beside me burned a lamp, and near it lay a little box. It was of no remarkable character, and I had seen it frequently before, for it was the property of the family physician; but how came it *there,* upon my table, and why did I shudder in regarding it? These things were in no manner to be accounted for, and my eyes at length dropped to the open pages of a book, and to a sentence underscored therein. The words were the singular but simple ones of the poet Ebn Zaiat:—"*Dicebant mihi sodales si sepulchrum amicæ visitarem, curas meas aliquantulum fore levatas.*" Why, then, as I perused them, did the hairs of my head erect themselves on end, and the blood of my body become congealed within my veins?

There came a light tap at the library door—

and, pale as the tenant of a tomb, a menial entered upon tiptoe. His looks were wild with terror, and he spoke to me in a voice tremulous, husky, and very low. What said he?—some broken sentences I heard. He told of a wild cry disturbing the silence of the night—of the gathering together of the household—of a search in the direction of the sound; and then his tones grew thrillingly distinct as he whispered me of a violated grave—of a disfigured body enshrouded, yet still breathing—still palpitating—*still alive!*

He pointed to my garments; they were muddy and clotted with gore. I spoke not, and he took me gently by the hand: it was indented with the impress of human nails. He directed my attention to some object against the wall. I looked at it for some minutes: it was a spade. With a shriek I bounded to the table, and grasped the box that lay upon it. But I could not force it open; and, in my tremor, it slipped from my hands, and fell heavily, and burst into pieces; and from it, with a rattling sound, there rolled out some instruments of dental surgery, intermingled with thirty-two small, white, and ivory-looking substances that were scattered to and fro about the floor.

ELEONORA

[Published in *The Gift*, 1842.]

Sub conservatione formæ specificæ salva anima.
—*Raymond Lully.*

I AM come of a race noted for vigor of fancy and ardor of passion. Men have called me mad; but the question is not yet settled, whether madness is or is not the loftiest intelligence—whether much that is glorious—whether all that is profound—does not spring from disease of thought—from *moods* of mind exalted at the expense of the general intellect. They who dream by day are cognizant of many things which escape those who dream only by night. In their gray visions they obtain glimpses of eternity, and thrill, in waking, to find that they have been upon the verge of the great secret. In snatches, they learn something of the wisdom which is of good, and more of the mere knowledge which is of evil. They penetrate, however, rudderless or compassless into the vast ocean of the "light ineffable," and again, like the adventures of the Nubian geographer, "*agressi sunt mare tenebrarum, quid in eo esset exploraturi.*"

We will say, then, that I am mad. I grant, at least, that there are two distinct conditions of my mental existence—the condition of a lucid reason, not to be disputed, and belonging to the memory of events forming the first epoch of my life—and a condition of shadow and doubt, appertaining to the present, and to the recollection of what constitutes the second great era of my being. Therefore, what I shall tell of the earlier period, believe; and to what I may relate of the later time, give only such credit as may seem due; or doubt it altogether; or, if doubt it ye cannot, then play unto its riddle the Œdipus.

She whom I loved in youth, and of whom I now pen calmly and distinctly these remembrances, was the sole daughter of the only sister of my mother long departed. Eleonora was the name of my cousin. We had always dwelled together, beneath a tropical sun, in the Valley of the Many-Colored Grass. No unguided footstep ever came upon that vale; for it lay far away up among a range of giant hills that hung beetling around about it, shutting out the sunlight from its sweetest recesses. No path was trodden in its vicinity; and, to reach our happy home, there was a need of putting back, with force the foliage of many thousands of forest trees, and of crushing to death the glories of many millions of fragrant flowers. Thus it was that we lived all alone, knowing nothing of the world without the valley,—I, and my cousin, and her mother.

From the dim regions beyond the mountains at the upper end of our encircled domain, there crept out a narrow and deep river, brighter than all save the eyes of Eleonora; and, winding stealthily about in mazy courses, it passed away, at length, through a shadowy gorge, among hills still dimmer than those whence it had issued. We called it the "River of Silence;" for there seemed to be a hushing influence in its flow. No murmur arose from its bed, and so gently it wandered along, that the pearly pebbles upon which we loved to gaze, far down within its bosom, stirred not at all, but lay in a motionless content, each in its own old station, shining on gloriously forever.

The margin of the river, and of the many dazzling rivulets that glided through devious ways into its channel, as well as the spaces that extended from the margins away down into the depths of the streams until they reached the bed of pebbles at the bottom,—these spots, not less than the whole surface of the valley, from the river to the mountains that girdled it in, were carpeted all by a soft green grass, thick, short, perfectly even, and vanilla-perfumed, but so besprinkled throughout with the yellow buttercup, the white daisy, the purple violet, and the ruby-red asphodel, that its exceeding beauty spoke to our hearts in loud tones, of the love and of the glory of God.

And, here and there, in groves about this grass, like wildernesses of dreams, sprang up fantastic trees, whose tall slender stems stood not upright, but slanted gracefully toward the light that peered at noon-day into the centre of the valley. Their bark was speckled with the vivid alternate splendor of ebony and silver, and was smoother than all save the cheeks of Eleonora; so that, but for the brilliant green of the huge leaves that spread from their summits in long, tremulous lines, dallying with the Zephyrs, one might have fancied them giant serpents of Syria doing homage to their Sovereign the Sun.

Hand in hand about this valley, for fifteen years, roamed I with Eleonora before Love entered within our hearts. It was one evening at the close of the third lustrum of her life, and of the fourth of my own, that we sat, locked in each other's embrace, beneath the serpent-like trees, and looked down within the waters of the River of Silence at our images therein. We spoke no words during the rest of that sweet day; and our words even upon the morrow were tremulous and few. We had drawn the god Eros from that wave, and now we felt that he had enkindled within us the fiery souls of our forefathers. The passions which had for centuries distinguished our race, came thronging with the fancies for which they had been equally noted, and together breathed a delirious bliss over the Valley of the Many-Colored Grass. A change fell upon all things. Strange, brilliant flowers, star-shaped, burst out upon the trees where no flowers had been known before. The tints of the green carpet deepened; and when, one by one, the white daisies shrank away, there sprang up in place of them, ten by ten of the ruby-red asphodel. And life arose in our paths; for the tall flamingo, hitherto unseen, with all gay glowing birds, flaunted his scarlet plumage before us. The golden and silver fish haunted the river, out of the bosom of which issued, little by little, a murmur that swelled, at length, into a lulling melody more divine than that of the harp of Æolus—sweeter than all save the voice of Eleonora. And now, too, a voluminous cloud, which we had long watched in the regions of Hesper, floated out thence, all gorgeous in crimson and gold, and settling in peace above us, sank, day by day, lower and lower, until its edges rested upon the tops of the mountains, turning all their dimness into magnificence, and shutting us up, as if forever, within a magic prison-house of grandeur and of glory.

The loveliness of Eleonora was that of the Seraphim; but she was a maiden artless and innocent as the brief life she had led among the flowers. No guile disguised the fervor of love which animated her heart, and she examined with me its innermost recesses as we walked together in the Valley of the Many-Colored Grass, and discoursed of the mighty changes which had lately taken place therein.

At length, having spoken one day, in tears, of the last sad change which must befall Humanity, she thenceforward dwelt only upon this one sorrowful theme, interweaving it into all our converse, as, in the songs of the bard of Schiraz, the same images are found occurring, again and again, in every impressive variation of phrase.

She had seen that the finger of Death was upon her bosom—that, like the ephemeron, she had been made perfect in loveliness only to die; but the terrors of the grave to her lay solely in a consideration which she revealed to me, one evening at twilight, by the banks of the River of Silence. She grieved to think that, having entombed her in the Valley of the Many-Colored Grass, I would quit forever its happy recesses, transferring the love which now was so passionately her own to some maiden of the outer and every-day world. And, then and there, I threw myself hurriedly at the feet of Eleonora, and offered up a vow, to herself and to Heaven, that I would never bind myself in marriage to any daughter of Earth—that I would in no manner prove recreant to her dear memory, or to the memory of the devout affection with which she had blessed me. And I called the Mighty Ruler of the Universe to witness the pious solemnity of my vow. And the curse which I invoked of *Him* and of her, a saint in Helusion, should I prove traitorous to that promise, involved a penalty the exceeding great horror of which will not permit me to make record of it here. And the bright eyes of Eleonora grew brighter at my words; and she sighed as if a deadly burthen had been taken from her breast; and she trembled and very bitterly wept; but she made acceptance of the vow, (for what was she but a child?) and it made easy to her the bed of her death. And she said to me, not many days afterward, tranquilly dying, that, because of what I had done for the comfort of her spirit she would watch over me in that spirit when departed, and, if so it were permitted her, return to me visibly in the watches of the night; but, if this thing were, indeed, beyond the power of the souls in Paradise, that she would, at least, give me frequent indications of her presence; sighing upon me in the evening winds, or filling the air which I breathed with perfume from the censers of the angels. And, with these words upon her lips, she yielded up her innocent life, putting an end to the first epoch of my own.

Thus far I have faithfully said. But as I pass the barrier in Time's path, formed by the death of my beloved, and proceed with the second era of my existence, I feel that a shadow gathers over my brain, and I mistrust the perfect sanity of the record. But let me on.—Years dragged themselves along heavily, and still I dwelled within the Valley of the Many-Colored Grass; but a second change had come upon all things. The star-shaped flowers shrank into the stems of the trees, and appeared no more. The tints of the green carpet faded; and, one by one, the ruby-red asphodels withered away; and there sprang up, in place of them, ten by ten, dark, eye-like violets, that writhed uneasily and were ever encumbered with dew. And Life departed from our paths; for the tall flamingo flaunted no longer his scarlet plumage before us, but flew sadly from the vale into the hills, with all the gay glowing birds that had arrived in his company. And the golden and silver fish swam down through the gorge at the lower end of our domain and bedecked the sweet river never again. And the lulling melody that had been softer than the wind-harp of Æolus, and more divine than all save the voice of Eleonora, it died little by little away, in murmurs growing lower and lower, until the stream returned, at length, utterly into the solemnity of its original silence. And then, lastly, the voluminous cloud uprose, and, abandoning the tops of the mountains to the dimness of old, fell back into the regions of Hesper, and took away all its manifold golden and gorgeous glories from the Valley of the Many-Colored Grass.

Yet the promises of Eleonora were not forgotten; for I heard the sounds of the swinging of the censers of the angels; and streams of a holy perfume floated ever and ever about the valley; and at lone hours, when my heart beat heavily, the winds that bathed my brow came unto me laden with soft sighs; and indistinct murmurs filled often the night air; and once—oh, but once only! I was awakened from a slumber, like the slumber of death, by the pressing of spiritual lips upon my own.

But the void within my heart refused, even thus, to be filled. I longed for the love which had before filled it to overflowing. At length the valley *pained* me through its memories of Eleonora, and I left it for ever for the vanities and the turbulent triumphs of the world.

* * * * * * *

I found myself within a strange city, where all things might have served to blot from recollection the sweet dreams I had dreamed so long in the Valley of the Many-Colored Grass. The pomps and pageantries of a stately court, and the mad clangor of arms, and the radiant loveliness of women, bewildered and intoxicated my brain. But as yet my soul had proved true to its vows, and the indications of the presence of Eleonora were still given me in the silent hours of the night. Suddenly these manifestations they ceased, and the world grew dark before mine eyes, and I stood aghast at the burning thoughts which possessed, at the terrible temptations which beset me; for there came from some far, far distant and unknown land, into the gay court of the king I served, a maiden to whose beauty my whole recreant heart yielded at once—at whose footstool I bowed down without a struggle, in the most ardent, in the most abject worship of love. What, indeed, was my passion for the young girl of the valley in comparison with the fervor, and the delirium, and the spirit-lifting ecstasy of adoration with which I poured out my whole soul in tears at the feet of the ethereal Ermengarde? Oh, bright was the seraph Ermengarde! and in that knowledge I had room for none other. Oh, divine was the angel Ermengarde! and as I looked down into the depths of her memorial eyes, I thought only of them—and *of her*.

I wedded,—nor dreaded the curse I had invoked; and its bitterness was not visited upon me. And once—but once again in the silence of the night—there came through my lattice the soft sighs which had forsaken me; and they modelled themselves into familiar and sweet voice, saying:

"Sleep in peace! for the Spirit of Love reigneth and ruleth, and, in taking to thy passionate heart her who is Ermengarde, thou art absolved, for reasons which shall be made known to thee in Heaven, of thy vows unto Eleonora."

LIGEIA

[Published in the *American Museum*, September, 1838.]

And the will therein lieth, which dieth not. Who knoweth the mysteries of the will, with its vigor? For God is but a great will pervading all things by nature of its intentness. Man doth not yield himself to the angels, nor unto death utterly, save only through the weakness of his feeble will.—*Joseph Glanvill.*

I CANNOT, for my soul, remember how, when, or even precisely where, I first became acquainted with the lady Ligeia. Long years have since elapsed, and my memory is feeble through much suffering. Or, perhaps, I cannot *now* bring these points to mind, because, in truth, the character of my beloved, her rare learning, her singular yet placid cast of beauty, and the thrilling and enthralling eloquence of her low musical language, made their way into my heart by paces so steadily and stealthily progressive, that they have been unnoticed and unknown. Yet I believe that I met her first and most frequently in some large, old, decaying city near the Rhine. Of her family—I have surely heard her speak. That it is of a remotely ancient date cannot be doubted. Ligeia! Ligeia! Buried in studies of a nature more than all else adapted to deaden impressions of the outward world, it is by that sweet word alone—by Ligeia—that I bring before mine eyes in fancy the image of her who is no more. And now, while I write, a recollection flashes upon me that I have *never known* the paternal name of her who was my friend and my betrothed, and who became the partner of my studies, and finally the wife of my bosom. Was it a playful charge on the part of my Ligeia? or was it a test of my strength of affection, that I should institute no inquiries upon this point? or was it rather a caprice of my own—a wildly romantic offering on the shrine of the most passionate devotion? I but indistinctly recall the fact itself—what wonder that I have utterly forgotten the circumstances which originated or attended it? And, indeed, if ever that spirit which is entitled *Romance*—if ever she, the wan and the misty-winged *Ashtophet* of idolatrous Egypt, presided, as they tell, over marriages ill-omened, then most surely she presided over mine.

There is one dear topic, however, on which my memory fails me not. It is the *person* of Ligeia. In stature she was tall, somewhat slender, and, in her latter days, even emaciated. I would in vain attempt to portray the majesty, the quiet ease of her demeanor, or the incomprehensible lightness and elasticity of her footfall. She came and departed as a shadow. I was never made aware of her entrance into my closed study, save by the dear music of her low sweet voice, as she placed her marble hand upon my shoulder. In beauty of face no maiden ever equalled her. It was the radiance of an opium-dream—an airy and spirit-lifting vision more wildly divine than the phantasies which hovered about the slumbering souls of the daughters of Delos. Yet her features were not of that regular mould which we have been falsely taught to worship in the classical labors of the heathen. "There is no exquisite beauty," says Bacon, Lord Verulam, speaking truly of all the forms and *genera* of beauty, "without some *strangeness* in the proportion." Yet, although I saw that the features of Ligeia were not of a classic regularity—although I perceived that her loveliness was indeed "exquisite," and felt that there was much of "strangeness" pervading it, yet I have tried in vain to detect the irregularity and to trace home my own perception of "the strange." I examined the contour of the lofty and pale forehead—it was faultless—how cold indeed that word when applied to a majesty so divine!—the skin rivalling the purest ivory, the commanding extent and repose, the gentle prominence of the regions above the temples; and then the raven-black, the glossy, the luxuriant, and naturally-curling tresses, setting forth the full force of the Homeric epithet, "hyacinthine!" I looked at the delicate outlines of the nose—and nowhere but in the graceful medallions of the Hebrews had I beheld a similar perfection. There were the same luxurious smoothness of surface, the same scarcely perceptible tendency to the aquiline, the same harmoniously curved nostrils speaking the free spirit. I regarded the sweet mouth. Here was indeed the triumph of all things heavenly—the magnificent turn of the short upper lip—the soft, voluptuous slumber of the under—the dimples which sported, and the color which spoke—the teeth glancing back, with a brilliancy almost startling, every ray of the holy light which fell upon them in her serene and placid yet most exultingly radiant of all smiles. I scrutinized the formation of the chin—and, here too, I found the gentleness of breadth, the softness and the majesty, the fulness and the spirituality, of the Greek—the contour which the god Apollo revealed but in a dream, to Cleomenes, the son of the Athenian. And then I peered into the large eyes of Ligeia.

For eyes we have no models in the remotely antique. It might have been, too, that in these eyes of my beloved lay the secret to which Lord Verulam alludes. They were, I must believe, far larger than the ordinary eyes of our own race. They were even fuller than the fullest of the gazelle eyes of the tribe of the valley of Nourjahad. Yet it was only at intervals—in moments of intense excitement—that this peculiarity became more than slightly noticeable in Ligeia. And at such moments was her beauty—in my heated fancy thus it appeared perhaps—the beauty of beings either above or apart from the earth—the beauty of the fabulous Houri of the Turk. The hue of the orbs was the most brilliant of black, and, far over them, hung jetty lashes of great length. The brows, slightly irregular in outline, had the same tint. The "strangeness," however, which I found in the eyes was of a nature distinct from the formation, or the color, or the brilliancy of the features, and must, after all, be referred to the *expression*. Ah, word of no meaning! behind whose vast latitude of mere sound we intrench our ignorance of so much of the spiritual. The expression of the eyes of Ligeia! How for long hours have I pondered upon it! How have I, through the whole of a midsummer night, struggled to fathom it! What was it—that something more profound than the well of Democritus—which lay far within the pupils of my beloved? What *was* it? I was possessed with a passion to discover. Those eyes! those large, those shining, those divine orbs! they became to me twin stars of Leda, and I to them devoutest of astrologers.

There is no point, among the many incomprehensible anomalies of the science of mind, more thrillingly exciting than the fact—never, I believe, noticed in the schools—than in our endeavors to recall to memory something long forgotten, we often find ourselves *upon the very verge* of remembrance, without being able, in the end, to remember. And thus how frequently, in my intense scrutiny of Ligeia's eyes, have I felt approaching the full knowledge of their expression—felt it approaching—yet not quite be mine—and so at length entirely depart! And (strange, oh, strangest mystery of all!) I found, in the commonest objects of the universe, a circle of analogies to that expression. I mean to say that, subsequently to the period when Ligeia's beauty passed into my spirit, there dwelling as in a shrine, I derived, from many existences in the material world, a sentiment such as I felt always around, within me, by her large and luminous orbs. Yet not the more could I define that sentiment, or analyze, or even steadily view it. I recognized it, let me repeat, sometimes in the survey of a rapidly growing vine—in the contemplation of a moth, a butterfly, a chrysalis, a stream of running water. I have felt it in the ocean—in the falling of a meteor. I have felt it in the glances of unusually aged people. And there are one or two stars in heaven (one especially, a star of the sixth magnitude, double and changeable, to be found near the large star in Lyra) in a telescopic scrutiny of which I have been made aware of the feeling. I have been filled with it by certain sounds from stringed instruments, and not unfrequently by passages from books. Among innumerable other instances, I well remember something in a volume of Joseph Glanvill, which (perhaps merely from its quaintness—who shall say?) never failed to inspire me with the sentiment: "And the will therein lieth, which dieth not. Who knoweth the mysteries of the will, with its vigor? For God is but a great will pervading all things by nature of its intentness. Man doth not yield him to the angels, nor unto death utterly, save only through the weakness of his feeble will."

Length of years and subsequent reflection have enabled me to trace, indeed, some remote connection between this passage in the English moralist and a portion of the character of Ligeia. An *intensity* in thought, action, or speech was possibly, in her, a result, or at least an index, of that gigantic volition which, during our long intercourse, failed to give other and more immediate evidence of its existence. Of all the women whom I have ever known, she, the outwardly calm, the ever-placid Ligeia, was the most violently a prey to the tumultuous vultures of stern passion. And of such passion I could form no estimate, save by the miraculous expansion of those eyes which at once so delighted and appalled me,—by the almost magical melody, modulation, distinctness, and placidity of her very low voice,—and by the fierce energy (rendered doubly effective by contrast with her manner of utterance) of the wild words which she habitually uttered.

I have spoken of the learning of Ligeia: it was immense—such as I have never known in woman. In the classical tongues was she deeply proficient, and as far as my own acquaintance extended in regard to the modern dialects of Europe, I have never known her at fault. Indeed upon any theme of the most admired because simply the most abstruse of the boasted erudition of the Academy, have I *ever* found Ligeia at fault? How singularly—how thrillingly, this one point in the nature of my wife has forced itself, at this late period only, upon my attention! I said her knowledge was such as I have never known in woman—but where breathes the man who has traversed, and successfully, *all* the wide areas of moral, physical, and mathematical science? I saw not then what I now clearly perceive that the acquisitions of Ligeia were gigantic, were astounding; yet I was sufficiently aware of her infinite supremacy to resign myself, with a child-like confidence, to her guidance through the chaotic world of metaphysical investigation at which I was most busily occupied during the earlier years of our marriage. With how vast a triumph—with how vivid a delight—with how much of all that is ethereal in hope did I *feel*, as she bent over me in studies but little sought—but less known,—that delicious vista by slow degrees expanding before me, down whose long, gorgeous, and all untrodden path, I might at length pass onward to the goal of a wisdom too divinely precious not to be forbidden.

How poignant, then, must have been the grief with which, after some years, I beheld my well-grounded expectations take wings to themselves and fly away! Without Ligeia I was but as a child groping benighted. Her presence, her readings alone, rendered vividly luminous the many mysteries of the transcendentalism in which we were immersed. Wanting the radiant lustre of her eyes, letters, lambent and golden, grew duller than Saturnian lead. And now those eyes shone less and less frequently upon the pages over which I pored. Ligeia grew ill. The wild eyes blazed with a too—too glorious effulgence; the pale fingers became of the transparent waxen hue of the grave; and the blue veins upon the lofty forehead swelled and sank impetuously with the tides of the most gentle emotion. I saw that she must die—and I struggled desperately in spirit with the grim Azrael. And the struggles of the passionate wife were, to my astonishment, even more energetic than my own. There had been much in her stern nature to impress me with the belief that, to her, death would have come without its terrors; but not so. Words are impotent to convey any just idea of the fierceness of resistance with which she wrestled with the Shadow. I groaned in anguish at the pitiable spectacle. I would have soothed—I would have reasoned; but in the intensity of her wild desire for life—for life—*but* for life—solace and reason were alike the uttermost of folly. Yet not until the last instance, amid the most convulsive writhings of her fierce spirit, was shaken the external placidity of her demeanor. Her voice grew more gentle—grew more low—yet I would not wish to dwell upon the wild meaning of the quietly uttered words. My brain reeled as I hearkened, entranced, to a melody more than mortal—to assumptions and aspirations which mortality had never before known.

That she loved me I should not have doubted; and I might have been easily aware that, in a bosom such as hers, love would have reigned no ordinary passion. But in death only was I fully impressed with the strength of her affection. For long hours, detaining my hand, would she pour out before me the overflowing of a heart whose more than passionate devotion amounted to idolatry. How had I deserved to be so blessed by such confessions?—how had I deserved to be so cursed with the removal of my beloved in the hour of my making them? But upon this subject I cannot bear to dilate. Let me say only, that in Ligeia's more than womanly abandonment to a love, alas! all unmerited, all unworthily bestowed, I at length, recognized the principle of her longing, with so wildly earnest a desire, for the life which was now fleeing so rapidly away. It is this wild longing—it is this eager vehemence of desire for life—*but* for life—that I have no power to portray—no utterance capable of expressing.

At high noon of the night in which she departed, beckoning me, peremptorily, to her side, she bade me repeat certain verses composed by herself not many days before. I obeyed her. They were these:—

Lo! 'tis a gala night
  Within the lonesome latter years!
An angel throng, bewinged, bedight
  In veils, and drowned in tears,
Sit in a theatre, to see
  A play of hopes and fears,
While the orchestra breathes fitfully
  The music of the spheres.

Mimes, in the form of God on high,
  Mutter and mumble low,
And hither and thither fly;
  Mere puppets they, who come and go
At bidding of vast formless things
  That shift the scenery to and fro,
Flapping from out their condor wings
  Invisible Wo!

That motley drama!—oh, be sure
  It shall not be forgot!
With its Phantom chased for evermore
  By a crowd that seize it not,
Through a circle that ever returneth in
  To the self-same spot;
And much of Madness, and more of Sin
  And Horror, the soul of the plot!

But see, amid the mimic rout,
  A crawling shape intrude!
A blood-red thing that writhes from out
  The scenic solitude!
It writhes!—it writhes!—with mortal pangs
  The mimes become its food,
And the seraphs sob at vermin fangs
  In human gore imbued.

Out—out are the lights—out all!
  And over each quivering form,
The curtain, a funeral pall,
  Comes down with the rush of a storm—
And the angels, all pallid and wan,
  Uprising, unveiling, affirm
That the play is the tragedy, "Man,"
  And its hero, the conqueror Worm.

"O God!" half shrieked Ligeia, leaping to her feet and extending her arms aloft with a spasmodic movement, as I made an end of these lines—"O God! O Divine Father!—shall these things be undeviatingly so?—shall this conqueror be not once conquered? Are we not part and parcel in Thee? Who—who knoweth the mysteries of the will with its vigor? Man doth not yield him to the angels, *nor unto death utterly*, save only through the weakness of his feeble will."

And now, as if exhausted with emotion, she suffered her white arms to fall, and returned solemnly to her bed of death. And as she breathed her last sighs, there came mingled with them a low murmur from her lips. I bent to them my ear, and distinguished, again, the concluding words of the passage in Glanvill: "*Man doth not yield him to the angels, nor unto death utterly, save only through the weakness of his feeble will.*"

She died: and I, crushed into the very dust with sorrow, could no longer endure the lonely desolation of my dwelling in the dim and decaying city by the Rhine. I had no lack of what the world calls wealth. Ligeia had brought me far more, very far more, than ordinarily falls to the lot of mortals. After a few months, therefore, of weary and aimless wandering, I purchased and put in some repair, an abbey, which I shall not name, in one of the wildest and least frequented portions of fair England. The gloomy and dreary grandeur of the building, the almost savage aspect of the domain, the many melancholy and time-honored memories connected with both, had much in unison with the feelings of utter abandonment which had driven me into that remote and unsocial region of the country. Yet although the external abbey, with its verdant decay hanging about it, suffered but little alteration, I gave way, with a child-like perversity, and perchance with a faint hope of alleviating my sorrows, to a display of more than regal magnificence within. For such follies, even in childhood, I had imbibed a taste, and now they came back to me as if in the dotage of grief. Alas, I feel how much even of incipient madness might have been discovered in the gorgeous and fantastic draperies, in the solemn carvings of Egypt, in the wild cornices and furniture, in the Bedlam patterns of the carpets of tufted gold! I had become a bounden slave in the trammels of opium, and my labors and my orders had taken a coloring from my dreams. But these absurdities I must not pause to detail. Let me speak only of that one chamber, ever accursed, whither, in a moment of mental alienation, I led from the altar as my bride—as the successor of the unforgotten Ligeia—the fair-haired and blue-eyed Lady Rowena Trevanion, of Tremaine.

There is no individual portion of the architecture and decoration of that bridal chamber which is not now visibly before me. Where were the souls of the haughty family of the bride, when, through thirst of gold, they permitted to pass the threshold of an apartment *so* bedecked, a maiden and a daughter so beloved? I have said, that I minutely remember the details of the chamber—yet I am sadly forgetful on topics of deep moment; and here there was no system, no keeping, in the fantastic display, to take hold upon the memory. The room lay in a high turret of the castellated abbey, was pentagonal in shape, and of capacious size. Occupying the whole southern face of the pentagon was the sole window—an immense sheet of unbroken glass from Venice—a single pane, and tinted of a leaden hue, so that the rays of either the sun or moon passing through it, fell with a ghastly lustre on the objects within. Over the upper portion of this huge window, extended the trelliswork of an aged vine, which clambered up the massy walls of the turret. The ceiling, of gloomy-looking oak, was excessively lofty, vaulted, and elaborately fretted with the wildest and most grotesque specimens of a semi-Gothic, semi-Druidical device. From out the most central recess of this melancholy vaulting, depended, by a single chain of gold with long links, a huge censer of the same metal, Saracenic in pattern, and with many perforations so contrived that there writhed in and out of them, as if endued with a serpent vitality, a continual succession of parti-colored fires.

Some few ottomans and golden candelabra, of Eastern figure, were in various stations about; and there was the couch, too—the bridal couch—of an Indian model, and low, and sculptured of solid ebony, with a pall-like canopy above. In each of the angles of the chamber stood on end a gigantic sarcophagus of black granite, from the tombs of the kings over against Luxor, with their aged lids full of immemorial sculpture. But in the draping of the apartment lay, alas! the chief phantasy of all. The lofty walls, gigantic in height—even unproportionably so—were hung from summit to foot, in vast folds, with a heavy and massive-looking tapestry—tapestry of a material which was found alike as a carpet on the floor, as a covering for the ottomans and the ebony bed, as a canopy for the bed, and as the gorgeous volutes of the curtains which partially shaded the window. The material was the richest cloth of gold. It was spotted all over, at irregular intervals, with arabesque figures, about a foot in diameter, and wrought upon the cloth in patterns of the most jetty black. But these figures partook of the true character of the arabesque only when regarded from a single point of view. By a contrivance now common, and indeeed traceable to a very remote period of antiquity, they were made changeable in aspect. To one entering the room, they bore the appearance of simple monstrosities; but upon a farther advance, this appearance gradually departed; and, step by step, as the visitor moved his station in the chamber, he saw himself surrounded by an endless succession of the ghastly forms which belong to the superstition of the Norman, or arise in the guilty slumbers of the monk. The phantasmagoric effect was vastly heightened by the artificial introduction of a strong continual current of wind behind the draperies—giving a hideous and uneasy animation to the whole.

In halls such as these—in a bridal chamber such as this—I passed, with the Lady of Tremaine, the unhallowed hours of the first month of our marriage—passed them with but little disquietude. That my wife dreaded the fierce moodiness of my temper—that she shunned me, and loved me but little—I could not help perceiving; but it gave me rather pleasure than otherwise. I loathed her with a hatred belonging more to demon than to man. My memory flew back (oh, with what intensity of regret!) to Ligeia, the beloved, the august, the beautiful, the entombed. I revelled in recollections of her purity, of her wisdom, of her lofty—her ethereal nature, of her passionate, her idolatrous love. Now, then, did my spirit fully and freely burn with more than all the fires of her own. In the excitement of my opium dreams (for I was habitually fettered in the shackles of the drug), I would call aloud upon her name, during the silence of the night, or among the sheltered recesses of the glens by day, as if, through the wild eagerness, the solemn passion, the consuming ardor of my longing for the departed, I could restore her to the pathways she had abandoned—ah, *could* it be for ever?—upon the earth.

About the commencement of the second month of the marriage, the Lady Rowena was attacked with sudden illness, from which her recovery was slow. The fever which consumed her rendered her nights uneasy; and in her perturbed state of half-slumber, she spoke of sounds, and of motions, in and about the chamber of the turret, which I concluded had no origin save in the distemper of her fancy, or perhaps in the phantasmagoric influences of the chamber itself. She became at length convalescent—finally, well. Yet but a brief period elapsed, ere a second more violent disorder again threw her upon a bed of suffering; and from this attack her frame, at all times feeble, never altogether recovered. Her illnesses were, after this epoch, of alarming character, and of more alarming recurrence, defying alike the knowledge and the great exertions of her physicians. With the increase of the chronic disease, which had thus, apparently, taken too sure hold upon her constitution to be eradicated by human means, I could not fail to observe a similar increase in the nervous irritation of her temperament, and in her excitability by trivial causes of fear. She spoke again, and now more frequently and pertinaciously, of the sounds—of the slight sounds—and of the unusual motions among the tapestries, to which she had formerly alluded.

One night, near the closing in of September, she pressed this distressing subject with more than usual emphasis upon my attention. She had just awakened from an unquiet slumber, and I had been watching, with feelings half of anxiety, half of vague terror, the workings of her emaciated countenance. I sat by the side of her ebony bed, upon one of the ottomans of India. She partly arose, and spoke, in an earnest low whisper, of sounds which she *then* heard, but which I could not hear—of motions which she *then* saw, but which I could not perceive. The wind was rushing hurriedly behind the tapestries, and I wished to show her (what, let me confess it, I could not *all* believe) that those almost inarticulate breathings, and those very gentle variations of the figures upon the wall, were but the natural effects of that customary rushing of the wind. But a deadly pallor, overspreading her face, had proved to me that my exertions to reassure her would be fruitless. She appeared to be fainting, and no attendants were within call. I remembered where was deposited a decanter of light wine which had been ordered by her physicians, and hastened across the chamber to procure it. But, as I stepped beneath the light of the censer, two circumstances of a startling nature attracted my attention. I had felt that some palpable although invisible object had passed lightly by my person; and I saw that there lay upon the golden carpet, in the very middle of the rich lustre thrown from the censer, a shadow—a faint, indefinite shadow of angelic aspect—such as might be fancied for the shadow of a shade. But I was wild with the excitement of an immoderate dose of opium, and heeded these things but little, nor spoke of them to Rowena. Having found the wine, I recrossed the chamber, and poured out a gobletful, which I held to the lips of the fainting lady. She had now partially recovered, however, and took the vessel herself, while I sank upon an ottoman near me, with my eyes fastened upon her person. It was then that I became distinctly aware of a gentle foot-fall upon the carpet, and near the couch; and in a second thereafter, as Rowena was in the act of raising the wine to her lips, I saw, or may have dreamed that I saw, fall within the goblet, as if from some invisible spring in the atmosphere of the room, three or four large drops of a brilliant and ruby colored fluid. If this I saw—not so Rowena. She swallowed the wine unhesitatingly, and I forebore to speak to her of a circumstance which must, after all, I considered, have been but the suggestion of a vivid imagination, rendered morbidly active by the terror of the lady, by the opium, and by the hour.

Yet I cannot conceal it from my own perception that, immediately subsequent to the fall of the ruby-drops, a rapid change for the worse took place in the disorder of my wife; so that, on the third subsequent night, the hands of her menials prepared her for the tomb, and on the fourth, I sat alone, with her shrouded body, in that fantastic chamber which had received her as my bride. Wild visions, opium-engendered, flitted, shadow-like, before me. I gazed with unquiet eye upon the sarcophagi in the angles of the room, upon the varying figures of the drapery, and upon the writhing of the parti-colored fires in the censer overhead. My eyes then fell, as I called to mind the circumstances of a former night, to the spot beneath the glare of the censer where I had seen the faint traces of the shadow. It was there, however, no longer; and breathing with greater freedom, I turned my glances to the pallid and rigid figure upon the bed. Then rushed upon me a thousand memories of Ligeia—and then came back upon my heart, with the turbulent violence of a flood, the whole of that unutterable woe with which I had regarded *her* thus enshrouded. The night waned; and still, with a bosom full of bitter thoughts of the one only and supremely beloved, I remained gazing upon the body of Rowena.

It might have been midnight, or perhaps earlier, or later, for I had taken no note of time, when a sob, low, gentle, but very distinct, startled me from my revery. I *felt* that it came from the bed of ebony—the bed of death. I listened in an agony of superstitious terror—but there was no repetition of the sound. I strained my vision to detect any motion in the corpse—but there was not the slightest perceptible. Yet I could not have been deceived. I *had* heard the noise, however faint, and my soul was awakened within me. I resolutely and perseveringly kept my attention riveted upon the body. Many minutes elapsed before any circumstance occurred tending to throw light upon the mystery. At length it became evident that a slight, a very feeble, and barely noticeable tinge of color had flushed up within the cheeks, and along the sunken small veins of the eyelids. Through a species of unutterable horror and awe, for which the language of mortality has no sufficiently energetic expression, I felt my heart cease to beat, my limbs grow rigid where I sat. Yet a sense of duty finally operated to restore my self-possession. I could no longer doubt that we had been precipitate in our preparations—that Rowena still lived. It was necessary that some immediate exertion be made; yet the turret was altogether apart from the portion of the abbey tenanted by the servants—there were none within call—I had no means of summoning them to my aid without leaving the room for many minutes—and this I could not venture to do. I therefore struggled alone in my endeavors to call back the spirit still hovering. In a short period it was certain, however, that a relapse had taken place; the color disappeared from both eyelid and cheek, leaving a wanness even more than that of marble; the lips became doubly shrivelled and pinched up in the ghastly expression of death; a repulsive clamminess and coldness overspread rapidly the surface of the body; and all the usual rigorous stiffness immediately supervened. I fell back with a shudder upon the couch from which I had been so startlingly aroused, and again gave myself up to passionate waking visions of Ligeia.

An hour thus elapsed, when (could it be possible?) I was a second time aware of some vague sound issuing from the region of the bed. I listened—in extremity of horror. The sound came again—it was a sigh. Rushing to the corpse, I saw—distinctly saw—a tremor upon the lips. In a minute afterward they relaxed, disclosing a bright line of the pearly teeth. Amazement now struggled in my bosom with the profound awe which had hitherto reigned there alone. I felt that my vision grew dim, that my reason wandered; and it was only by a violent effort that I at length succeeded in nerving myself to the task which duty thus once more had pointed out. There was now a partial glow upon the forehead and upon the cheek and throat; a perceptible warmth pervaded the whole frame; there was even a slight pulsation at the heart. The lady *lived;* and with redoubled ardor I betook myself to the task of restoration. I chafed and bathed the temples and the hands, and used every exertion which experience, and no little medical reading, could suggest. But in vain. Suddenly, the color fled, the pulsation ceased, the lips resumed the expression of the dead, and, in an instant afterward, the whole body took upon itself the icy chilliness, the livid hue, the intense rigidity, the sunken outline, and all the loathsome peculiarities of that which has been, for many days, a tenant of the tomb.

And again I sunk into visions of Ligeia—and again, (what marvel that I shudder while I write?) *again* there reached my ears a low sob from the region of the ebony bed. But why shall I minutely detail the unspeakable horrors of that night? Why shall I pause to relate how, time after time, until near the period of the gray dawn, this hideous drama of revivification was repeated; how each terrific relapse was only into a sterner and apparently more irredeemable death; how each agony wore the aspect of a struggle with some invisible foe; and how each struggle was succeeded by I know not what of wild change in the personal appearance of the corpse? Let me hurry to a conclusion.

The greater part of the fearful night had worn away, and she who had been dead once again stirred—and now more vigorously than hitherto, although arousing from a dissolution more appalling in its utter hopelessness than any. I had long ceased to struggle or to move, and remained sitting rigidly upon the ottoman, a helpless prey to a whirl of violent emotions, of which extreme awe was perhaps the least terrible, the least consuming. The corpse, I repeat, stirred, and now more vigorously than before. The hues of life flushed up with unwonted energy into the countenance—the limbs relaxed—and, save that the eyelids were yet pressed heavily together, and that the bandages and draperies of the grave still imparted their charnel character to the figure, I might have dreamed that Rowena had indeed shaken off, utterly, the fetters of Death. But if this idea was not, even then, altogether adopted, I could at least doubt no longer, when, arising from the bed, tottering, with feeble steps, with closed eyes, and with the manner of one bewildered in a dream, the thing that was enshrouded advanced boldly and palpably into the middle of the apartment.

I trembled not—I stirred not—for a crowd of unutterable fancies connected with the air, the stature, the demeanor, of the figure, rushing hurriedly through my brain, had paralyzed—had chilled me into stone. I stirred not—but gazed upon the apparition. There was a mad disorder in my thoughts—a tumult unappeasable. Could it, indeed, be the *living* Rowena who confronted me? Could it, indeed, be Rowena *at all*—the fair-haired, the blue-eyed Lady Rowena Trevanion of Tremaine? Why, *why* should I doubt it? The bandage lay heavily about the mouth—but then might it not be the mouth of the breathing Lady of Tremaine? And the cheeks—there were the roses as in her noon of life—yes, these might indeed be the fair cheeks of the living Lady of Tremaine. And the chin, with its dimples, as in health, might it not be hers?—but *had she then grown taller since her malady?* What inexpressible madness seized me with that thought? One bound, and I had reached her feet! Shrinking from my touch, she let fall from her head, unloosened, the ghastly cerements which had confined it, and there streamed forth into the rushing atmosphere of the chamber huge masses of long and dishevelled hair; *it was blacker than the raven wings of midnight!* And now slowly opened *the eyes* of the figure which stood before me. "Here then, at least," I shrieked aloud, "can I never—can I never be mistaken—these are the full, and the black, and the wild eyes—of my lost love—of the Lady—of the LADY LIGEIA."

MORELLA

[Published in the *Southern Literary Messenger*, April, 1835.]

> *Αὐτὸ καθ' αὐτὸ μεθ' αὑτοῦ, μονοειδὲς ἀεὶ ὄν.*
> Itself, by itself solely, ONE everlastingly, and single.
> PLATO—*Sympos.*

WITH a feeling of deep yet most singular affection I regarded my friend Morella. Thrown by accident into her society many years ago, my soul, from our first meeting, burned with fires it had never before known; but the fires were not of Eros, and bitter and tormenting to my spirit was the gradual conviction that I could in no manner define their unusual meaning, or regulate their vague intensity. Yet we met; and fate bound us together at the altar; and I never spoke of passion, nor thought of love. She, however, shunned society, and, attaching herself to me alone, rendered me happy. It is a happiness to wonder;—it is a happiness to dream.

Morella's erudition was profound. As I hope to live, her talents were of no common order—her powers of mind were gigantic. I felt this, and, in many matters, became her pupil. I soon, however, found that, perhaps on account of her

Presburg education, she placed before me a number of those mystical writings which are usually considered the mere dross of the early German literature. These, for what reason I could not imagine, were her favorite and constant study—and that, in process of time, they became my own, should be attributed to the simple but effectual influence of habit and example.

In all this, if I err not, my reason had little to do. My convictions, or I forgot myself, were in no manner acted upon by the ideal, nor was any tincture of the mysticism which I read, to be discovered, unless I am greatly mistaken, either in my deeds or in my thoughts. Persuaded of this, I abandoned myself implicitly to the guidance of my wife, and entered with an unflinching heart into the intricacies of her studies. And then—then, when, poring over forbidden pages, I felt a forbidden spirit enkindling within me—would Morella place her cold hand upon my own, and rake up from the ashes of a dead philosophy some low, singular words, whose strange meaning burned themselves in upon my memory. And then, hour after hour, would I linger by her side, and dwell upon the music of her voice—until, at length, its melody was tainted with terror,—and there fell a shadow upon my soul—and I grew pale, and shuddered inwardly at those too unearthly tones. And thus, joy suddenly faded into horror, and the most beautiful became the most hideous, as Hinnon became Ge-Henna.

It is unnecessary to state the exact character

of those disquisitions which, growing out of the volumes I have mentioned, formed, for so long a time, almost the sole conversation of Morella and myself. By the learned in what might be termed theological morality they will be readily conceived, and by the unlearned they would at all events, be little understood. The wild Pantheism of Fichte; the modified *Παλιγγενεσία* of Pythagoreans; and, above all, the doctrines of *Identity* as urged by Schelling, were generally the points of discussion presenting the most of beauty to the imaginative Morella. That identity which is termed personal, Mr. Locke, I think, truly defines to consist in the saneness of a rational being. And since by person we understand an intelligent essence having reason, and since there is a consciousness which always accompanies thinking, it is this which makes us all to be that which we call *ourselves*—thereby distinguishing us from other beings that think, and giving us our personal identity. But the *principium individuationis*—the notion of that identity *which at death is or is not lost for ever*—was to me, at all times, a consideration of intense interest; not more from the perplexing and exciting nature of its consequences, than from the marked and agitated manner in which Morella mentioned them.

But, indeed, the time had now arrived when the mystery of my wife's manner oppressed me as a spell. I could no longer bear the touch of her wan fingers, nor the low tone of her musical language, ncr the lustre of her melancholy eyes. And she knew all this, but did not upbraid; she seemed conscious of my weakness or my folly, and, smiling, called it Fate. She seemed, also, conscious of a cause, to me unknown, for the gradual alienation of my regard; but she gave me no hint or token of its nature. Yet was she woman, and pined away daily. In time, the crimson spot settled steadily upon the cheek, and the blue veins upon the pale forehead became prominent; and, one instant, my nature melted into pity, but, in the next, I met the glance of her meaning eyes, and then my soul sickened and became giddy with the giddiness of one who gazes downward into some dreary and unfathomable abyss.

Shall I then say that I longed with an earnest and consuming desire for the moment of Morella's decease? I did; but the fragile spirit clung to its tenement of clay for many days—for many weeks and irksome months—until my tortured nerves obtained the mastery over my mind, and I grew furious through delay, and, with the heart of a fiend, cursed the days, and the hours, and the bitter moments, which seemed to lengthen and lengthen as her gentle life declined—like shadows in the dying of the day.

But one autumnal evening, when the winds lay still in heaven, Morella called me to her bedside. There was a dim mist over all the earth, and a warm glow upon the waters, and, amid the rich October leaves of the forest, a rainbow from the firmament had surely fallen.

"It is a day of days," she said, as I approached; "a day of all days either to live or die. It is a fair day for the sons of earth and life—ah, more fair for the daughters of heaven and death!"

I kissed her forehead, and she continued:

"I am dying, yet shall I live."

"Morella!"

"The days have never been when thou couldst love me—but her whom in life thou didst abhor, in death thou shalt adore."

"Morella!"

"I repeat that I am dying. But within me is a pledge of that affection—ah, how little! which thou didst feel for me, Morella. And when my spirit departs shall the child live—thy child and mine, Morella's. But thy days shall be days of sorrow—that sorrow which is the most lasting of impressions, as the cypress is the most enduring of trees. For the hours of thy happiness are over; and joy is not gathered twice in a life, as the roses of Pæstum twice in a year. Thou shalt no longer, then, play the Teian with time, but, being ignorant of the myrtle and the vine, thou shalt bear about with thee thy shroud on the earth, as do the Moslemin at Mecca."

"Morella!" I cried, "Morella! how knowest thou this?"—but she turned away her face upon the pillow, and, a slight tremor coming over her limbs, she thus died, and I heard her voice no more.

Yet, as she had foretold, her child—to which in dying she had given birth, which breathed not until the mother breathed no more—her child, a daughter, lived. And she grew strangely in stature and intellect, and was the perfect resemblance of her who had departed, and I loved her with a love more fervent than I had believed it possible to feel for any denizen of earth.

But, ere long, the heaven of this pure affection became darkened, and gloom, and horror, and grief, swept over it in clouds. I said the child grew strangely in stature and intelligence. Strange, indeed, was her rapid increase in bodily size—but terrible, oh! terrible were the tumultuous thoughts which crowded upon me while watching the development of her mental being! Could it be otherwise, when I daily discovered in the conceptions of the child the adult powers and faculties of the woman?—when the lessons of experience fell from the lips of infancy? and when the wisdom or the passions of maturity I found hourly gleaming from its full and speculative eye? When, I say, all this became evident to my appalled senses—when I could no longer hide it from my soul, nor throw it off from those preceptions which trembled to receive it—is it to be wondered at that suspicions, of a nature fearful and exciting, crept in upon my spirit, or that my thoughts fell back aghast, upon the wild tales and thrilling theories of the entombed Morella? I snatched from the scrutiny of the world a being whom destiny compelled me to adore, and in the rigorous seclusion of my home, watched with an agonizing anxiety over all which concerned the beloved.

And, as years rolled away, and I gazed, day

after day, upon her holy, and mild, and eloquent face, and pored over her maturing form, day, after day did I discover new points of resemblance in the child to her mother, the melancholy and the dead. And, hourly, grew darker these shadows of similitude, and more full, and more definite, and more perplexing, and more hideously terrible in their aspect. For that her smile was like her mother's I could bear; but then I shuddered at its too perfect *identity*—that her eyes were like Morella's I could endure; but then they too often looked down into the depths of my soul with Morella's own intense and bewildering meaning. And in the contour of the high forehead, and in the ringlets of the silken hair, and in the wan fingers which buried themselves therein, and in the sad musical tones of her speech, and above all—oh! above all—in the phrases and expressions of the dead on the lips of the loved and the living, I found food for consuming thought and horror—for a worm that *would* not die.

Thus passed away two lustra of her life, and, as yet, my daughter remained nameless upon the earth. "My child," and "my love," were the designations usually prompted by a father's affection, and the rigid seclusion of her days precluded all other intercourse. Morella's name died with her at her death. Of the mother I had never spoken to the daughter;—it was impossible to speak. Indeed, during the brief period of her existence, the latter had received no impressions from the outer world, save such as might have been afforded by the narrow limits of her privacy. But at length the ceremony of baptism presented to my mind, in its unnerved and agitated condition, a present deliverance from the terrors of my destiny. And at the baptismal fount I hesitated for a name. And many titles of the wise and beautiful, of old and modern times, of my own and foreign lands, came thronging to my lips, with many, many fair titles of the gentle and the happy, and the good. What prompted me, then, to disturb the memory of the buried dead? What demon urged me to breathe that sound, which, in its very recollection, was wont to make ebb the purple blood in torrents from the temples to the heart? What fiend spoke from the recesses of my soul, when, amid those dim aisles, and in the silence of the night, I whispered within the ears of the holy man the syllables—Morella? What more than fiend convulsed the features of my child, and overspread them with hues of death, as starting at that scarcely audible sound, she turned her glassy eyes from the earth to heaven, and, falling prostrate on the black slabs of our ancestral vault, responded—"I am here!"

Distinct, coldly, calmly distinct, fell those few simple sounds within my ear, and thence like molten lead, rolled hissingly into my brain. Years—years may pass away, but the memory of that epoch—never! Nor was I indeed ignorant of the flowers and the vine—but the hemlock and the cypress overshadowed me night and day. And I kept no reckoning of time or place, and the stars of my fate faded from heaven, and therefore the earth grew dark, and its figures passed by me, like flitting shadows, and among them all I beheld only—Morella. The winds of the firmament breathed but one sound within my ears, and the ripples upon the sea murmured evermore—Morella. But she died; and with my own hands I bore her to the tomb; and I laughed with a long and bitter laugh as I found no traces of the first, in the charnel where I laid the second, Morella.

THE ASSIGNATION

[Published in the *Southern Literary Messenger*, July, 1835, under the title of "The Visionary."]

Stay for me there! I will not fail
To meet thee in that hollow vale.

(*Exequy on the death of his wife, by Henry King, Bishop of Chichester.*)

Ill-fated and mysterious man!—bewildered in the brilliancy of thine own imagination, and fallen in the flames of thine own youth. Again in fancy I behold thee! Once more thy form hath risen before me!—not—oh! not as thou art —in the cold valley and shadow—but as thou *shouldst be*—squandering away a life of magnificent meditation in that city of dim visions, thine own Venice—which is a star-beloved Elysium of the sea, and the wide windows of whose Palladian palaces look down with a deep and bitter meaning upon the secrets of her silent waters. Yes! I repeat it—as thou *shouldst be*. There are surely other worlds than this—other thoughts than the thoughts of the multitude—other speculations than the speculations of the sophist. Who then shall call thy conduct into question? who blame thee for thy visionary hours, or denounce those occupations as a wasting away of life, which were but the overflowings of thine everlasting energies?

It was at Venice, beneath the covered archway there called the *Ponte di Sospiri,* that I met, for the third or fourth time the person of whom I speak. It is with a confused recollection that I bring to mind the circumstances of that meeting. Yet I remember—ah! how should I forget?—the deep midnight, the Bridge of Sighs, the beauty of woman, and the Genius of Romance that stalked up and down the narrow canal.

It was a night of unusual gloom. The great clock of the Piazza had sounded the fifth hour of the Italian evening. The square of the Campanile lay silent and deserted, and the lights in the old Ducal Palace were dying fast away. I was returning home from the Piazzetta, by way of the Grand Canal. But as my gondola arrived opposite the mouth of the canal San Marco, a female voice from its recesses broke suddenly upon the night, in one wild, hysterical, and long-continued shriek. Startled at the sound, I sprang upon my feet; while the gondolier, letting slip his single oar, lost it in the pitchy darkness beyond a chance of recovery, and we were consequently left to the guidance of the current which here sets from the greater into the smaller channel. Like some huge and sable-feathered condor, we were slowly drifting down toward the Bridge of Sighs, when a thousand flambeaux flashing from the windows, and down the staircases of the

Ducal Palace, turned all at once that deep gloom into a livid and preternatural day.

A child, slipping from the arms of its own mother, had fallen from an upper window of the lofty structure into the deep and dim canal. The quiet waters had closed placidly over their victim; and, although my own gondola was the only one in sight, many a stout swimmer, already in the stream, was seeking in vain upon the surface, the treasure which was to be found, alas! only within the abyss. Upon the broad black marble flagstones at the entrance of the palace, and a few steps above the water, stood a figure which none who then saw can have ever since forgotten. It was the Marchesa Aphrodite—the adoration of all Venice—the gayest of the gay—the most lovely where all were beautiful—but still the young wife of the old and intriguing Mentoni, and the mother of that fair child, her first and only one, who now, deep beneath the murky water, was thinking in bitterness of heart upon her sweet caresses, and exhausting its little life in struggles to call upon her name.

She stood alone. Her small, bare and silvery feet gleamed in the black mirror of marble beneath her. Her hair, not as yet more than half loosened for the night from its ball-room array, clustered, amid a shower of diamonds, round and round her classical head, in curls like those of the young hyacinth. A snowy-white and gauze-like drapery seemed to be nearly the sole covering to her delicate form; but the mid-summer and midnight air was hot, sullen, and still, and no motion in the statue-like form itself, stirred even the folds of that raiment of very vapor which hung around it as the heavy marble hangs around the Niobe. Yet—strange to say!—her large lustrous eyes were not turned downward upon that grave wherein her brightest hope lay buried—but riveted in a widely different direction! The prison of the Old Republic is, I think, the stateliest building in all Venice—but how could that lady gaze so fixedly upon it, when beneath her lay stifling, her own child? Yon dark, gloomy niche, too, yearns right opposite her chamber window—what, then, *could* there be in its shadows—in its architecture—in its ivy-wreathed and solemn cornices—that the Marchesa di Mentoni had not wondered at a thousand times before? Nonsense!—Who does not remember that, at such a time as this, the eye, like a shattered mirror, multiplies the images of its sorrow, and sees in innumerable far-off places, the woe which is close at hand?

Many steps above the Marchesa, and within the arch of the water-gate, stood, in full dress, the Satyr-like figure of Mentoni himself. He was occasionally occupied in thrumming a guitar, and seemed *ennuyé* to the very death, as at intervals he gave directions for the recovery of his child. Stupefied and aghast, I had myself no power to move from the upright position I had assumed upon first hearing the shriek, and must have presented to the eyes of the agitated group a spectral and ominous appearance, as with pale countenance and rigid limbs, I floated down among them in that funeral gondola.

All efforts proved in vain. Many of the most energetic in the search were relaxing their exertions, and yielding to a gloomy sorrow. There seemed but little hope for the child; (how much less than for the mother!) but now, from the interior of that dark niche which has been already mentioned as forming a part of the Old Republican prison, and as fronting the lattice of the Marchesa, a figure muffled in a cloak, stepped out within reach of the light, and, pausing a moment upon the verge of the giddy descent, plunged headlong into the canal. As, in an instant afterward, he stood with the still living and breathing child within his grasp, upon the marble flagstones by the side of the Marchesa, his cloak, heavy with the drenching water, became unfastened, and, falling in folds about his feet, discovered to the wonder-stricken spectators the graceful person of a very young man, with the sound of whose name the greater part of Europe was then ringing.

No word spoke the deliverer. But the Marchesa! She will now receive her child—she will press it to her heart—she will cling to its little form, and smother it with her caresses. Alas! *another's* arms have taken it from the stranger—*another's* arms have taken it away, and borne it afar off, unnoticed, into the palace! And the Marchesa! Her lip—her beautiful lip trembles; tears are gathering in her eyes—those eyes which, like Pliny's acanthus, are "soft and almost liquid.'' Yes! tears are gathering in those eyes—and see! the entire woman thrills throughout the soul, and the statue has started into life! The pallor of the marble countenance, the swelling of the marble bosom, the very purity of the marble feet, we behold suddenly flushed over with a tide of ungovernable crimson; and a slight shudder quivers about her delicate frame, as a gentle air at Napoli about the rich silver lilies in the grass.

Why *should* that lady blush. To this demand there is no answer—except that, having left, in the eager haste and terror of a mother's heart, the privacy of her own *boudoir*, she has neglected to enthral her tiny feet in their slippers, and utterly forgotten to throw over her Venetian shoulders that drapery which is their due. What other possible reason could there have been for her so blushing?—for the glance of those wild appealing eyes?—for the unusual tumult of that throbbing bosom?—for the convulsive pressure of that trembling hand?—that hand which fell, as Mentoni turned into the palace, accidentally, upon the hand of the stranger. What reason could there have been for the low—the singularly low tone of those unmeaning words which the lady uttered hurriedly in bidding him adieu? "Thou hast conquered," she said, or the murmurs of the water deceived me; "thou hast conquered—one hour after sunrise—we shall meet—so let it be!"

* * * * * * *

The tumult had subsided, the lights had died

away within the palace, and the stranger, whom I now recognized, stood alone upon the flags. He shook with inconceivable agitation, and his eye glanced around in search of a gondola. I could not do less than offer him the service of my own; and he accepted the civility. Having obtained an oar at the water-gate, we proceeded together to his residence, while he rapidly recovered his self-possession, and spoke of our former slight acquaintance in terms of great apparent cordiality.

There are some subjects upon which I take pleasure in being minute. The person of the stranger—let me call him by this title, who to all the world was still a stranger—the person of the stranger is one of these subjects. In height he might have been below rather than above the medium size: although there were moments of intense passion when his frame actually *expanded* and belied the assertion. The light, almost slender symmetry of his figure promised more of that ready activity which he had evinced at the Bridge of Sighs, than of that Herculean strength which he has been known to wield without an effort, upon occasions of more dangerous emergency. With the mouth and chin of a deity—singular, wild, full, liquid eyes, whose shadows varied from pure hazel to intense and brilliant jet—and a profusion of curling, black hair, from which a forehead of unusual breadth gleamed forth at intervals all light and ivory—his were features than which I have seen none more classically regular, except, perhaps, the marble ones of the Emperor Commodus. Yet his countenance was, nevertheless, one of those which all men have seen at some period of their lives, and have never afterward seen again. It had no peculiar, it had no settled predominant expression to be fastened upon the memory; a countenance seen and instantly forgotten, but forgotten with a vague and never-ceasing desire of recalling it to mind. Not that the spirit of each rapid passion failed, at any time, to throw its own distinct image upon the mirror of that face—but that the mirror, mirror-like, retained no vestige of the passion, when the passion had departed.

Upon leaving him on the night of our adventure, he solicited me, in what I thought an urgent manner, to call upon him *very* early the next morning. Shortly after sunrise, I found myself accordingly at his Palazzo, one of those huge structures of gloomy yet fantastic pomp, which tower above the waters of the Grand Canal in the vicinity of the Rialto. I was shown up a broad winding staircase of mosaics, into an apartment whose unparalleled splendor burst through the opening door with an actual glare, making me blind and dizzy with luxuriousness.

I knew my acquaintance to be wealthy. Report had spoken of his possessions in terms which I had even ventured to call terms of ridiculous exaggeration. But as I gazed about me, I could not bring myself to believe that the wealth of any subject in Europe could have supplied the princely magnificence which burned and blazed around.

Although, as I say, the sun had arisen, yet the room was still brilliantly lighted up. I judge from this circumstance, as well as from an air of exhaustion in the countenance of my friend, that he had not retired to bed during the whole of the preceding night. In the architecture and embellishments of the chamber, the evident design had been to dazzle and astound. Little attention had been paid to the *decora* of what is technically called *keeping*, or to the proprieties of nationality. The eye wandered from object to object, and rested upon none—neither the *grotesques* of the Greek painters, nor the sculptures of the best Italian days, nor the huge carvings of untutored Egypt. Rich draperies in every part of the room trembled to the vibration of low, melancholy music, whose origin was not to be discovered. The senses were oppressed by mingled and conflicting perfumes, reeking up from strange convolute censers, together with multitudinous flaring and flickering tongues of emerald and violet fire. The rays of the newly risen sun poured in upon the whole, through windows, formed each of a single pane of crimson-tinted glass. Glancing to and fro, in a thousand reflections, from curtains which rolled from their cornices like cataracts of molten silver, the beams of natural glory mingled at length fitfully with the artificial light, and lay weltering in subdued masses upon a carpet of rich, liquid-looking cloth of Chili gold.

"Ha! ha! ha!—ha! ha! ha!"—laughed the proprietor, motioning me to a seat as I entered the room, and throwing himself back at full-length upon an ottoman. "I see," said he, perceiving that I could not immediately reconcile myself to the *bienséance* of so singular a welcome,—"I see you are astonished at my apartment—at my statues—my pictures—my originality of conception in architecture and upholstery! absolutely drunk, eh, with my magnificence? But pardon me, my dear sir; (here his tone of voice dropped to the very spirit of cordiality,) pardon me for my uncharitable laughter. You appeared so *utterly* astonished. Besides, some things are so completely ludicrous, that a man *must* laugh, or die. To die laughing must be the most glorious of all glorious deaths! Sir Thomas More—a very fine man was Sir Thomas More—Sir Thomas More died laughing, you remember. Also in the 'Absurdities' of Ravisius Textor, there is a long list of characters who came to the same magnificent end. Do you know, however," continued he, musingly, "that at Sparta (which is now Palæochori), at Sparta, I say, to the west of the citadel, among a chaos of scarcely visible ruins, is a kind of *socle*, upon which are still legible the letters*ΑΑΣΜ*. They are undoubtedly part of *ΓΕΛΑΣΜΛ*. Now, at Sparta were a thousand temples and shrines to a thousand different divinities. How exceedingly strange that the altar of Laughter should have survived all the others! But in the present instance," he resumed, with a singular alteration of voice and manner, "I have no right to be merry at your expense. You might well have been amazed. Europe cannot produce any thing so fine as this, my little regal cabinet. My other apartments are by no means of the same order —mere *ultras* of fashionable insipidity. This is better than fashion—is it not? Yet this has but to be seen to become the rage—that is, with those who could afford it at the cost of their entire patrimony. I have guarded, however, against any such profanation. With one exception, you are the only human being, besides myself and my *valet*, who has been admitted within the mysteries of these imperial precincts, since they have been bedizened as you see!"

I bowed in acknowledgment—for the overpowering sense of splendor and perfume and music, together with the unexpected eccentricity of his address and manner, prevented me from expressing, in words, my appreciation of what I might have construed into a compliment.

"Here," he resumed, arising and leaning on my arm as he sauntered around the apartment, "here are paintings from the Greeks to Cimabue, and from Cimabue to the present hour. Many are chosen, as you see, with little deference to the opinions of Virtû. They are all, however, fitting tapestry for a chamber such as this. Here, too, are some *chefs-d'œuvre* of the unknown great; and here, unfinished designs by men, celebrated in their day, whose very names the perspicacity of the academies has left to silence and to me. What think you," said he, turning abruptly as he spoke,—"what think you of this Madonna della Pieta?"

"It is Guido's own!" I said, with all the enthusiasm of my nature, for I had been poring intently over its surpassing loveliness. "It is Guido's own!—how *could* you have obtained it? she is undoubtedly in painting what Venus is in sculpture."

"Ha!" said he, thoughtfully, "the Venus?—the beautiful Venus?—the Venus of the Medici?—she of the diminutive head and the gilded hair? Part of the left arm [here his voice dropped so as to be heard with difficulty], and all the right, are restorations, and in the coquetry of that right arm lies, I think, the quintessence of all affectation. Give *me* the Canova! The Apollo, too, is a copy—there can be no doubt of it—blind fool that I am, who cannot behold the boasted inspiration of the Apollo! I cannot help—pity me!—I cannot help preferring the Antinous. Was it not Socrates who said that the statuary found his statue in the block of marble? Then Michael Angelo was by no means original in his couplet—

> 'Non ha l'ottimo artista alcun concetto
> Che un marmo solo in se non circunscriva.' "

It has been, or should be remarked, that, in the manner of the true gentleman, we are always aware of a difference from the bearing of the vulgar, without being at once precisely able to determine in what such difference consists. Allowing the remark to have applied in its full force to the outward demeanor of my acquaintance, I felt it, on that eventful morning, still more fully applicable to his moral temperament and character. Nor can I better define that peculiarity of spirit which seemed to place him so essentially apart from all other human beings, than by calling it a *habit* of intense and continual thought, pervading even his most trivial actions—intruding upon his moments of dalliance—and interweaving itself with his very flashes of merriment—like adders which writhe from out the eyes of grinning masks in the cornices around the temples of Persepolis.

I could not help, however, repeatedly observing, through the mingled tone of levity and solemnity with which he rapidly descanted upon matters of little importance, a certain air of trepidation—a degree of nervous *unction* in action and in speech—an unquiet excitability of manner which appeared to me at all times unaccountable, and upon some occasions even filled me with alarm. Frequently, too, pausing in the middle of a sentence whose commencement he had apparently forgotten, he seemed to be listening in the deepest attention, as if either in momentary expectation of a visitor, or to sounds which must have had existence in his imagination alone.

It was during one of these reveries or pauses of apparent abstraction, that, in turning over a page of the poet and scholar Politian's beautiful tragedy, "The Orfeo" (the first native Italian tragedy), which lay near me upon an ottoman, I discovered a passage underlined in pencil. It was a passage toward the end of the third act—a passage of the most heart-stirring excitement—a passage which, although tainted with impurity, no man shall read without a thrill of novel emotion—no woman without a sigh. The whole page was blotted with fresh tears; and, upon the opposite interleaf, were the following English lines, written in a hand so very different from the peculiar characters of my acquaintance, that I had some difficulty in recognizing it as his own:

Thou wast that all to me, love,
  For which my soul did pine—
A green isle in the sea, love,
  A fountain and a shrine,
All wreathed with fairy fruits and flowers;
  And all the flowers were mine.

Ah, dream too bright to last!
  Ah, starry Hope, that didst arise
But to be overcast!
  A voice from out the Future cries,
"Onward!"—but o'er the Past
  (Dim gulf!) my spirit hovering lies,
Mute—motionless—aghast!

For alas! alas! with me
  The light of life is o'er.
  "No more—no more—no more,"
(Such language holds the solemn sea
To the sands upon the shore,)
  Shall bloom the thunder-blasted tree,
Or the stricken eagle soar!

Now all my hours are trances;
  And all my nightly dreams
Are where the dark eye glances,
  And where thy footstep gleams
In what ethereal dances,
  By what Italian streams.

Alas! for that accursed time
  They bore thee o'er the billow,
From Love to titled age and crime,
  And an unholy pillow!—
From me, and from our misty clime,
  Where weeps the silver willow!

That these lines were written in English—a language with which I had not believed their author acquainted—afforded me little matter for surprise. I was too well aware of the extent of his acquirements, and of the singular pleasure he took in concealing them from observation, to be astonished at any similar discovery; but the place of date, I must confess, occasioned me no little amazement. It had been originally *London,* and afterward carefully overscored—not, however, so effectually as to conceal the word from a scrutinizing eye. I say, this occasioned me no little amazement; for I well remember that, in a former conversation with my friend, I particularly inquired if he had at any time met in London the Marchesa di Mentoni (who for some years previous to her marriage had resided in that city), when his answer, if I mistake not, gave me to understand that he had never visited the metropolis of Great Britain. I might as well here mention, that I have more than once heard, (without, of course, giving credit to a report involving so many improbabilities,) that the person of whom I speak, was not only by birth, but in education, an *Englishman.*

* * * * * * *

"There is one painting," said he, without being aware of my notice of the tragedy,—"there is still one painting which you have not seen." And throwing aside a drapery, he discovered a full-length portrait of the Marchesa Aphrodite.

Human art could have done no more in the delineation of her superhuman beauty. The same ethereal figure which stood before me the preceding night upon the steps of the Ducal Palace, stood before me once again. But in the expression of the countenance, which was beaming all over with smiles, there still lurked (incomprehensible anomaly!) that fitful stain of melancholy which will ever be found inseparable from the perfection of the beautiful. Her right arm lay folded over her bosom. With her left she pointed downward to a curiously fashioned vase. One small, fairy foot, alone visible, barely touched the earth; and, scarcely discernible in the brilliant atmosphere which seemed to encircle and enshrine her loveliness, floated a pair of the most delicately imagined wings. My glance fell from the painting to the figure of my friend, and the vigorous words of Chapman's *Bussy D'Ambois*, quivered instinctively upon my lips:

> "He is up
> There like a Roman statue! He will stand
> Till Death hath made him marble!"

"Come," he said at length, turning toward a table of richly enamelled and massive silver, upon which were a few goblets fantastically stained, together with two large Etruscan vases, fashioned in the same extraordinary model as that in the foreground of the portrait, and filled with what I supposed to be Johannisberger. "Come," he said, abruptly, "let us drink! It is early—but let us drink. It is *indeed* early," he continued, musingly, as a cherub with a heavy golden hammer made the apartment ring with the first hour after sunrise: "It is *indeed* early —but what matters it? let us drink! Let us pour out an offering to yon solemn sun which these gaudy lamps and censers are so eager to subdue!" And having made me pledge him in a bumper, he swallowed in rapid succession several goblets of the wine.

"To dream," he continued, resuming the tone of his desultory conversation, as he held up to the rich light of a censer one of the magnificent vases—"to dream has been the business of my life. I have therefore framed for myself, as you see, a bower of dreams. In the heart of Venice could I have erected a better? You behold around you, it is true, a medley of architectural embellishments. The chastity of Ionia is offended by antediluvian devices, and the sphynxes of Egypt are outstretched upon carpets of gold. Yet the effect is incongruous to the timid alone. Properties of place, and especially of time, are the bugbears which terrify mankind from the contemplation of the magnificent. Once I was myself a decorist; but that sublimation of folly has palled upon my soul. All this is now the fitter for my purpose. Like these arabesque censers, my spirit is writhing in fire, and the delirium of this scene is fashioning me for the wilder visions of that land of real dreams whither I am now rapidly departing." He here paused abruptly, bent his head to his bosom, and seemed to listen to a sound which I could not hear. At length, erecting his frame, he looked upwards, and ejaculated the lines of the Bishop of Chichester:

> *"Stay for me there! I will not fail,*
> *To meet thee in that hollow vale."*

In the next instant, confessing the power of the wine, he threw himself at full length upon an ottoman.

A quick step was now heard upon the staircase, and a loud knock at the door rapidly succeeded. I was hastening to anticipate a second disturbance, when a page of Mentoni's household burst into the room, and faltered out, in a voice choking with emotion, the incoherent words, "My mistress! — my mistress! — Poisoned!— poisoned! Oh, beautiful—oh, beautiful Aphrodite!"

Bewildered, I flew to the ottoman, and endeavored to arouse the sleeper to a sense of the startling intelligence. But his limbs were rigid— his lips were livid—his lately beaming eyes were riveted in *death.* I staggered back toward the table—my hand fell upon a cracked and blackened goblet—and a consciousness of the entire and terrible truth flashed suddenly over my soul.

THE OVAL PORTRAIT

[Published in *Graham's Magazine*, April, 1842.]

The château into which my valet had ventured to make forcible entrance, rather than permit me, in my desperately wounded condition, to pass a night in the open air, was one of those piles of commingled gloom and grandeur which have so long frowned among the Appennines, not less in fact than in the fancy of Mrs. Radcliffe. To all appearance it had been temporarily and very lately abandoned. We established ourselves in one of the smallest and least sumptuously furnished apartments. It lay in a remote turret of the building. Its decorations were rich, yet tattered and antique. Its walls were hung with tapestry and bedecked with manifold and multiform armorial trophies, together with an unusually great number of very spirited modern paintings in frames of rich golden arabesque. In these paintings, which depended from the walls not only in their main surfaces, but in very many nooks which the bizarre architecture of the château rendered necessary—in these paintings my incipient delirium, perhaps, had caused me to take deep interest; so that I bade Pedro to close the heavy shutters of the room—since it was already night,—to light the tongues of a tall candelabrum which stood by the head of the bed, and to throw open far and wide the fringed curtains of black velvet which enveloped the bed itself. I wished all this done that I might resign myself, if not to sleep, at least alternately to the contemplation of these pictures, and the perusal of a small volume which had been found upon the pillow, and which purported to criticise and describe them.

Long, long I read—and devoutly, devotedly I gazed. Rapidly and gloriously the hours flew by and the deep midnight came. The position of the candelabrum displeased me, and outreaching my hand with difficulty, rather than disturb my slumbering valet, I placed it so as to throw its rays more fully upon the book.

But the action produced an effect altogether unanticipated. The rays of the numerous candles (for there were many) now fell within a niche of the room which had hitherto been thrown into deep shade by one of the bed-posts. I thus saw in vivid light a picture all unnoticed before. It was the portrait of a young girl just ripening into womanhood. I glanced at the painting hurriedly, and then closed my eyes. Why I did this was not at first apparent even to my own perception. But while my lids remained thus shut, I ran over in mind my reason for so shutting them. It was an impulsive movement to gain time for thought—to make sure that my vision had not deceived me—to calm and subdue my fancy for a more sober and more certain gaze. In a very few moments I again looked fixedly at the painting.

That I now saw aright I could not and would not doubt; for the first flashing of the candles upon that canvas had seemed to dissipate the dreamy stupor which was stealing over my senses, and to startle me at once into waking life.

The portrait, I have already said, was that of a young girl. It was a mere head and shoulders, done in what is technically termed a *vignette* manner; much in the style of the favorite heads of Sully. The arms, the bosom, and even the ends of the radiant hair melted imperceptibly into the vague yet deep shadow which formed the background of the whole. The frame was oval, richly gilded and filagreed in *Moresque*. As a thing of art nothing could be more admirable than the painting itself. But it could have been neither the execution of the work, nor the immortal beauty of the countenance, which had so suddenly and so vehemently moved me. Least of all, could it have been that my fancy, shaken from its half slumber, had mistaken the head for that of a living person. I saw at once that the peculiarities of the design, of the *vignetting*, and of the frame, must have instantly dispelled such idea—must have prevented even its momentary entertainment. Thinking earnestly upon these points, I remained, for an hour perhaps, half sitting, half reclining, with my vision riveted upon the portrait. At length, satisfied with the true secret of its effect, I fell back within the bed. I had found the spell of the picture in an absolute *life-likeliness* of expression, which, at first startling, finally confounded, subdued, and appalled me. With deep and reverent awe I replaced the candelabrum in its former position. The cause of my deep agitation being thus shut from view, I sought eagerly the volume which discussed the paintings and their histories. Turning to the number which designated the oval portrait, I there read the vague and quaint words which follow:

She was a maiden of rarest beauty, and not more lovely than full of glee. And evil was the hour when she saw, and loved, and wedded the painter. He, passionate, studious, austere, and having already a bride in his Art: she a maiden of rarest beauty, and not more lovely than full of glee; all light and smiles, and frolicsome as the young fawn; loving and cherishing all things; hating only the Art which was her rival; dreading only the pallet and brushes and other untoward instruments which deprived her of the countenance of her lover. It was thus a terrible thing for this lady to hear the painter speak of his desire to portray even his young bride. But she was humble and obedient, and sat meekly for many weeks in the dark high turret-chamber where the light dripped upon the pale canvas only from overhead. But he, the painter, took glory in his work, which went on from hour to hour, and from day to day. And he was a passionate, and wild, and moody man, who became lost in reveries; so that he *would* not see that the light which fell so ghastly in that lone turret withered the health and the spirits of his bride, who pined visibly to all but him. Yet she smiled on and still on, uncomplainingly, because she saw that the painter (who had high renown) took a fervid and burning pleasure in his task, and wrought day and night to depict her who so loved him, yet who grew daily more dispirited and weak. And in sooth some who beheld the portrait spoke of its resemblance in low words, as of a mighty marvel, and a proof not less of the power of the painter than of his deep love for her whom he depicted so surpassingly well. But at length, as the labor drew nearer to its conclusion, there were admitted none into the turret; for the painter had grown wild with the ardor of his work, and turned his eyes from the canvas rarely, even to regard the countenance of his wife. And he *would* not see that the tints which he spread upon the canvas were drawn from the cheeks of her who sat beside him. And when many weeks had passed, and but little remained to do, save one brush upon the mouth and one tint upon the eye, the spirit of the lady again flickered up as the flame within the socket of the lamp. And then the brush was given, and then the tint was placed; and, for one moment, the painter stood entranced before the work which he had wrought; but in the next, while he yet gazed, he grew tremulous and very pallid, and aghast, and crying with a loud voice, 'This is indeed *Life* itself!' turned suddenly to regard his beloved:—*She was dead!*"

SHADOW—A PARABLE

[Published in the *Southern Literary Messenger*, September, 1835.]

Yea! though I walk through the valley of the *Shadow.*
—*Psalm of David.*

YE who read are still among the living; but I who write shall have long since gone my way into the region of shadows. For indeed strange things shall happen, and secret things be known, and many centuries shall pass away, ere these memorials be seen of men. And, when seen, there will be some to disbelieve, and some to doubt, and yet a few who will find much to ponder upon in the character here graven with a stylus of iron.

The year had been a year of terror, and of feelings more intense than terror for which there is no name upon the earth. For many prodigies and signs had taken place, and far and wide, over sea and land, the black wings of the Pestilence were spread abroad. To those, nevertheless, cunning in the stars, it was not unknown that the heavens wore an aspect of ill; and to me, the Greek Oinos, among others, it was evident that now had arrived the alternation of that seven hundred and ninety-fourth year when, at the entrance of Aries, the planet Jupiter is conjoined with the red ring of the terrible Saturnus. The peculiar spirit of the skies, if I mistake not greatly, made itself manifest, not only in the physical orb of the earth, but in the souls, imaginations, and meditations of mankind.

Over some flasks of the red Chian wine, within the walls of a noble hall, in a dim city called Ptolemais, we sat, at night, a company of seven. And to our chamber there was no entrance save by a lofty door of brass: and the door was fashioned by the artisan Corinnos, and, being of rare workmanship, was fastened from within. Black draperies, likewise, in the gloomy room, shut out from our view the moon, the lurid stars, and the peopleless streets—but the boding and the memory of Evil, they would not be so excluded. There were things around us and about of which I can render no distinct account—things material and spiritual—heaviness in the atmosphere—a sense of suffocation—anxiety—and, above all, that terrible state of existence which the nervous experience when the senses are keenly living and awake, and meanwhile the powers of thought lie dormant. A dead weight hung upon us. It hung upon our limbs—upon the household furniture—upon the goblets from which we drank; and all things were depressed, and borne down thereby—all things save only the flames of the seven iron lamps which illuminated our revel.

tones of any one being, but of a multitude of beings, and, varying in their cadences from syllable to syllable, fell duskly upon our ears in the well-remembered and familiar accents of many thousand departed friends.

Poe

Works of Edgar Allan Poe